CONVERTING the
PREACHER'S
Heart

OTHER BOOKS BY LORIN GRACE

AMERICAN HOMESPUN SERIES
Waking Lucy
Remembering Anna
Reforming Elizabeth
Healing Sarah

ARTISTS & BILLIONAIRES
Mending Fences
Mending Christmas
Mending Walls
Mending Images
Mending Words
Mending Hearts

HASTINGS SECURITY
Not the Bodyguard's Baby
Not the Bodyguard's Widow
Not the Bodyguard's Boss
Not the Bodyguard's Princess
Not the Bodyguard's Bride

MISADVENTURES IN LOVE
Miss Guided
Miss Oriented

SPELLBOUND IN HAWTHORNE
(with Maria Hoagland)
Taste of Memory
Sprinkle of Snow
Hint of Charm
Dash of Destiny
Stir of Wind
Essence of Gravity

BRADFORD BRIDES
Rescuing the Sheriff's Heart
Bending the Blacksmith's Heart
Converting the Preacher's Heart
Healing the Doctor's Heart

HASTINGS LEGACY
Too Much in Common

STAND ALONE TITLES
A Little Clean Fun
Love in the Valley

Lorin Grace

MARA

THANKS FOR KEEPING ME WRITING.

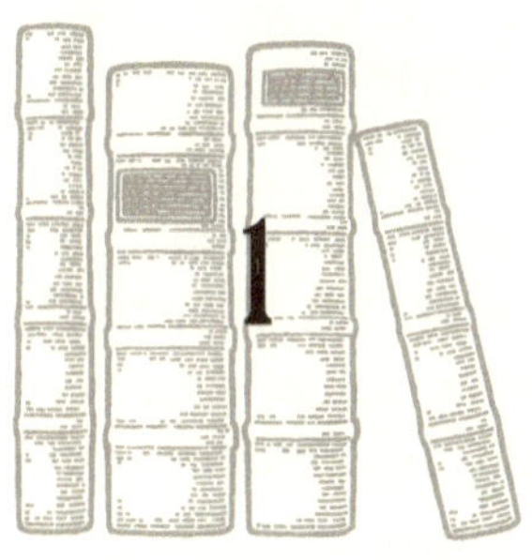

July 1879

Thirty-seven yards.

Years ago, Lewis and his best friend Clifford measured the distance between their neighboring homes. They'd climbed the fence dividing the yards so often their fathers added a gate between the properties. The children had dashed from one house to the other through the kitchen doors, causing the cooks to yell and withhold treats and the maids to threaten them with brooms. Clifford's twin sisters had swung on the gate until it broke, leaving a gap that was never closed.

Today wasn't a back door day.

Never had the walk from his front door to the Taylor's been longer. With each step, the distance expanded. Maybe it was thirty-seven hundred yards.

Lewis stopped at the picket gate guarding the Taylor's front walk and stared up at the newly repainted three-story mansion. His parents would paint theirs next. No one in their Brookline, Massachusetts neighborhood wanted to appear behind the times. The tree that had stolen his kite twenty years ago shaded the front yard. With no little girls to pick them for crowns, flowers grew in abundance in the manicured beds edging the home. Instead of laughter, silence filled the shade.

A few streets over, the train to Boston blew its whistle, reminding commuters to hurry. In five days, it would be the first of many trains to call him as he traveled to Texas. There, he would take his first post since graduating from the seminary two months ago.

The whistle blew again. Only five days. He must hurry to secure a bride. At the very least, a fiancée. If he failed, church leadership would demote him from junior minister to clerk.

Last fall, the Taylor twins had started at Bradford College. Renowned for graduating the first female foreign missionary, the school was the perfect training ground for a minister's wife. Either twin could fill the role nicely. Playful Catherine had a quick smile and made friends wherever she went. Quiet Clara challenged him with her questions that made him stretch his mind and cared for all around her. For weeks, he'd prayed to be led to choosing the right twin to share his life.

Last evening, after a long conversation at the annual Independence Day picnic, he felt Clara would be the best wife for a minster, even if she didn't have Catherine's talent for charming people and mingling in large groups.

What if he chose wrong?

What if it should be Catherine?

He turned the knob to ring the bell. Waiting for the butler to answer, Lewis stepped back and straightened his tie, and then took a deep breath. His heart raced faster than a train. He raised his hand to ring again when the door opened.

Lewis froze. Which sister stood before him? When they were younger, Mrs. Taylor often dressed the twins the same but with different hair ribbons in their blond hair, so the staff and everyone else could tell them apart. Although Catherine convinced Clara to switch hair ribbons often.

The white garden dress with black trim was not either woman's preferred color. Clara often chose blue over Catherine's red. Jewelry. Catherine always wore a necklace and earrings where Clara only wore jewelry of any kind when forced to and often fiddled with it.

The neck of the woman in front of him was bare of chains or broaches.

Lewis removed his hat and cleared his throat. "May I have a moment of your time, Miss Taylor?"

"Of course. Would you like to sit in the parlor or on the porch swing?"

"The parlor." He didn't want the neighbors to witness his proposal.

The twin led the way into the room decorated in the latest style, almost exactly like his parents' parlor. She adjusted her skirts and sat on the settee. Instead of pointing to the chair opposite, she patted the vacant cushion beside her. Lewis checked again to be sure he spoke to the right sister. If only one had a mole on her cheek or a scar, any identifying mark to confirm his deductions. No jewelry, no half smile, back ramrod straight in perfect posture. She had to be Clara.

He paused one last time. Was he making a mistake? His sister claimed all women desired a love match, a notion that had little place for an effective modern clergyman. They were fond friends, and if he allowed her the last year of Bradford College to polish her talents and refinements, they would have time to come to know each other's hopes and aspirations through letters.

Clara smiled up at him, then averted her eyes, playing with the handkerchief she'd embroidered last summer. Yes, he'd made the correct choice. A preacher's wife should be demure, like Clara.

Lewis dropped to one knee and faced her. "I know this is unexpected, since we have not courted. However, I have every reason to believe we suit. I leave in five days and I cannot leave without knowing your answer." He took a breath. He was rambling. "Marry me?"

"Yes!" She leaned forward and threw her arms around his neck, plastering a kiss on his lips.

Lewis grabbed her arms so as to not fall over from his kneeling position. Clara was full of surprises this afternoon. Once steady, he wrapped his arms around her and kissed her back, sealing the proposal.

"Catherine? Catherine?" A voice floated through the doorway.

The woman in his arms stiffened. They pulled back simultaneously before the speaker discovered them in an embrace. He had yet to speak to her father. A faux pas he would soon rectify.

"There you are. Lewis, why are you kneeling? Catherine, wha—" The real Clara's voice faltered as her eyes widened. She spun on one heel, her skirts lifting enough to show a set of scuffed boots so unlike the shiny new ones near his knee.

Lewis stood. How had he proposed to the wrong twin?

2

No, Clara, that belongs in my trunk." Catherine lay on the fainting couch in their bedroom, directing the last of the packing.

For days, Clara had bit her tongue at her sister's demands. Catherine wasn't the only one moving to Texas. Clara held up the doily, one of two dozen Catherine had received as wedding gifts. "What does it matter? We will be in the same town."

"Aunt Lillian gave it to me."

Clara tossed the lace circle in one of Catherine's trunks. How could her sister remember which of the doilies came from whom? Most of them looked as identical as the sisters did. Now they had a new distinction. Clara was no longer just Catherine's twin. She was the one who hadn't made a proper match yet. Perhaps she'd find some cowboy or lawman in Texas, like her friend Emily had. Surely someone could like her for herself and not the fact that she was Catherine's twin.

5

Clara tossed another doily into the largest of the four trunks.

"Be careful," snapped Catherine.

"Stop telling me what to do. I'm trying to help, and once again you're sitting there acting like you are queen bee because you're getting married"—*to the man I thought I'd marry*— "and I am only to be a teacher." Clara tried to calm her voice before her sister found something new to snap at.

"I'm sorry. I am so nervous. I appreciate you coming with me. You are giving up so much. The parties and balls, the trips to the Cape. Not to mention most of the Independence Day festivities. It is most unfair that we cannot wait another week. Lewis's superiors are so fastidious, and one year apparently means exactly 365 days and not a second more, leap year or not."

An exaggeration, and they both knew it. They would be on the train on July fifth, the anniversary of the proposal. From Lewis's letters, the church leadership was quite anxious to see him wed. Clara wasn't clear on all the reasons, avoiding feuds within the congregation when young women vied for a minister's hand was only part of their reasoning.

"Don't fret on my account. I don't care for Boston society like you do." Waiting wouldn't make witnessing Lewis marry Catherine any easier. She would lose her sister and her friend in one day. Although she'd really lost him last year when he proposed—a proposal that baffled her. Only the night before, she and Lewis had discussed points of Martin Luther's Hymn *"Dies sind die heilgen zehn Gebot"* on the Ten Commandments, which didn't have a popular English translation. They'd shared an ice cream and, and… It wasn't fair. Until the day of the proposal, Catherine and Lewis had hardly spoken beyond pleasantries. At least not that her sister had mentioned, or she herself had observed. Lewis had never been one of Catherine's many beaux. Lewis should have proposed to her, not Catherine. Everyone always loved her vivacious sister more.

Clara turned so her sister couldn't see her face. One of the worst things about being a twin was that lying was nearly impossible. Catherine almost always knew. Perhaps because Catherine was much better at falsehoods than she was. Since the day Lewis made his choice, Clara had lived a lie; pretending to be happy for Catherine while concealing her own heart. Every letter Catherine read out loud hurt a little more. Clara's only consolation was that Lewis never wrote that he loved Catherine or closed with flowery terms of endearment.

"It is rude for Bernard not to write."

Her sister's sudden change in conversation caused Clara to drop the stocking she was rolling. She'd accompanied Bernard on several occasions. However, he never proposed or even suggested summer plans. Truthfully, she only accompanied the man to show her friends at school she was not jealous of Catherine's engagement.

"Have you heard from Bernard at all since graduation?" Catherine continued to press the subject.

The answer was the same as last week. "No."

"I really thought there might be something…" Catherine let the thought float between them.

"Bernard was only marking time with me. He talked to you more often." The only thing she had to remember the year-long flirtation with, on his part more than Clara's, was the journal and a note wishing her safe travels he'd given her for a graduation gift. He'd given Catherine a similar journal in blue rather than red, getting their current favorite colors confused—a fact that should hurt more than it did. Clara wouldn't have seen him so often if it hadn't been for trying to heal her broken heart over Lewis. It hadn't worked. Bernard only praised her beauty and never her intellect, even when she'd helped him with his philosophy class. After the night when she refused Bernard's kiss, she'd avoided being alone with him.

"Did it hurt very much?"

Clara folded a set of pillowcases. "Did what hurt?"

"Losing Bernard?"

"I don't think I ever had him." Considering how often he mixed them up, he didn't even know her.

Clara tucked the pillowcases around her traditional white graduation dress. Several of her friends had used theirs as wedding dresses before cutting them down to make baptismal dresses for their babies, a dream Clara secretly cherished for the simple silk gown. Even if she inherited Catherine's wedding dress, Clara would wear her white graduation dress. Pearls and lace were all well and fine, but there was something elegant about simplicity.

Mother bustled in to check the trunks. "Anything missing? I can send someone to R.H. White's."

Catherine toyed with a scrap of linen remaining after the maid had wrapped their best gowns. "I've already had to leave behind more than I wish. My china…"

"Which we will send when you need it. Lewis's mother said his congregation was very poor. You don't want to put on airs around them. A minister's wife should be above such things." Mother picked up one of Clara's books. "You should take fewer books. They make the trunks so heavy."

"I am only taking the necessary ones. Emily Morgan has gathered an extensive library in the few months since she started the school, but she has only two German texts and little in the way of science."

"I am not entirely sure it is proper to teach at a school full of fallen women." Mother frowned. She'd been of two minds ever since Clara received the invitation to teach. One moment, Mother encouraged Clara to spread her wings, the next she lamented Clara entering the working world. The line between respectable and charitable overlapped.

"Mother, these are the same type of women your benevolent society wants to help. Education is the key to giving women more choices in their life. Besides, everyone agreed it would be best if Catherine and I traveled together. You even said it was positively providential that Lewis was assigned to the same town where my friend lives."

Mother put her hand over her heart. "I'm so afraid that you will succumb to some unlawfulness, like your friend. Or worse, marry a cowboy or lawman."

If only she could be so fortunate—to marry, not to succumb to some unlawfulness. She preferred to avoid kidnapping and debauchery. Clara laughed to lighten the mood. "You read another of those dime novels, didn't you? Emily's husband is still the sheriff and Hiramsville is growing more civilized each day."

"She only writes those things to entice you to come." Mother hovered over Catherine's second trunk.

"Lewis says the same, does he not, Catherine?"

"Hmm? Oh yes. He writes Hiramsville is quite civilized. The manse is modernized, with an indoor toilet and tub as fine as ours." Clara had been as surprised as Catherine at the fine house provided to the congregation's minister. She'd expected a rustic log cabin.

A maid appeared in the doorway with a worn leather satchel in her arms. "Mrs. Staples sent this over. She said the reverend asked for it in his last letter."

Catherine wrinkled her nose. "Clara, be a dear and make room in your trunks for that."

"It belongs to Lewis. You should take it. I can take some of your doilies and linens."

"But you have room." Catherine's voice raised a notch. "Mother, tell her."

"Girls." Mother wore her exasperated look, which came immediately before her what-is-a-mother-to-do look. "Clara, tuck it in your trunk. You should stop calling him Lewis. What will the town's people think of you being so familiar with their minister?"

"I've known him my entire life, and he will be my brother-in-law." Calling him Reverend Lewis Staples would be as if she hardly knew him at all. Perhaps given the state of her locked heart, it was better that she call him by a more formal name. Clara rearranged some of her books to accommodate the satchel.

Father's heavy footfalls vibrated the floor as he came down the hall to the room. "There are my girls."

Mother turned her cheek for a kiss. "You are home early."

"Yes. I had lunch with Mr. Ashford, and he mentioned that he wished he'd sent his daughter with enough money to return home if she needed to. So I went to the bank and brought you each ten double eagle coins. Mr. Ashford suggested coins since some of the banks were hesitant to take notes from Northern institutions."

Two hundred dollars was enough money to return to Boston twice over.

"Put them in the lining of your corsets, dears. It will keep train robbers from finding them." Mother's advice was not new. Clara already had fifty dollars in coins sewn into her corset. The addition of the double eagles would be enough to protect her like an armored knight.

"Mother, dime novels are fiction." Clara held out her hand for her coins. "However, if it eases your mind, I will keep mine in my corset."

"No need. I can carry your money. I sewed a special pouch in my underskirt for it." Catherine held out both hands.

Father gave Clara her coins. "Catherine, you need to stop taking care of Clara. It is high time she learns to do things for herself."

Clara's jaw clenched to contain all the words she wanted to say. Who always picked up after Catherine and reminded her of the simplest things? Who cajoled Catherine into completing her studies? Who cleaned their dorm room for inspections?

"Of course, Father." Catherine took her coins.

"Hurry and finish, girls. Mrs. Staples is coming for tea to say her final goodbyes."

As soon as their parents left, Catherine sat back down on the fainting couch. "Tea with Mrs. Staples again?"

"She will be your mother-in-law. I think she wants the connection with her son. It is terribly hard on all of them being denied witnessing your wedding." Mrs. Staples's rheumatism acted up in the heat, and a days-long train ride wasn't an option. Mother felt it wouldn't be fair for the Taylors to attend if the Staples could not.

"I do so wish Lewis could have come back to Boston to be married. It would have been so lovely. All of our friends would be there."

"And all your friends could be green with envy over your dress," said Clara.

"That too." Catherine giggled.

"If we don't finish packing, we will both be missing your wedding in Texas." Clara folded another pair of stockings to fill the space between the larger items.

Catherine stacked her coins beside her. "You're sure I can't carry your money?"

Did her own sister think she was that gullible? By age five, she'd learned never to trust Catherine with anything she considered valuable. "It's best if we each have our own money. If something were to happen or we become separated, we will need our own."

"How can that happen? Don't tell me you've been reading mother's dime novels."

"No, I have not. Even if I had, I know they are only stories." Stories with happy endings for the good guys. Happy endings that didn't occur in real life.

<hr>

The walk to the Hiramsville Post Office took Lewis twice as long as any other man as he was obliged to stop and talk to every person he met on his way. This morning, everyone was out taking care of an errand they didn't want to run later in the day when the sun burned down on them.

"How do you do, Mrs. Reese?" She was one of the few people he didn't mind stopping to talk with. The widowed matron held sway over the entire town and did more good than a convent of nuns. It was her word which convinced the church committee, here and in Austin, that he was ready to take Reverend Green's place when he became too ill to continue.

"Right as rain, Reverend Staples. Is your bride on her way?" Mrs. Reese carried a basket of goods, likely for a family in need or for the Rescue.

"Her father wired. The twins left Boston this morning. She should be here Friday evening." He would be married the following Wednesday—only a week and a half away. The time came faster than he thought.

"I have a room all ready for her sister. I suppose they will both stay with me for the first few nights until you are wed." Mrs. Reese shared her large home with an occasional boarder or strays, as she called them.

"Yes. Thank you so much for offering to put them up." Without a proper boarding house in town, Lewis was going to have to pay for a hotel room. Hannah, the hotel manager, offered him a discount on a room. Still, every penny he saved from his meager salary was dear to him.

"No bother at all, Reverend. I'm thrilled Emily will have

a teacher at Rose's Rescue to help her." Mrs. Reese fanned herself. "I need to finish my errands. Have a good day."

If only everyone ended their conversations with him as quickly. One theological question and two how-do-you-dos later, Lewis entered the post office.

"Got one of those fancy letters for you, Preacher. Probably the last one seeing as how your bride is on the train." Mr. Penny searched through the pigeon holes behind him.

Lewis's head popped up. He was about to ask how the postmaster knew about Catherine and Clara's arrival, then realized Mr. Penny occasionally filled in for Mr. Saunders at the telegraph office. Hiramsville's true source of gossip wasn't the quilting circle.

The postmaster handed over a letter addressed in Catherine's familiar hand and another one from his mother.

Lewis returned to the manse before opening either letter. His mother's missive was full of her regret that she could not be at his wedding and no less than four reminders to have a photographer take a photo of them in their fancy clothes.

Catherine's letter began with her normal update on how many wedding gifts they'd received and how she had to return another piece of crystal. After a year, her missives were no more personal than if she'd written a stranger. Catherine rarely shared her opinion on anything, even when he asked. For months, he told himself the proposal mix up must be God's will. Her kisses had been enthusiastic enough to make him hope for closeness in their marriage. Years stretched ahead with a woman who treated him at best like a brother, at least in conversation.

Clara had long since stopped writing to him, even questions ecclesiastical in nature. He hoped to maintain their friendship since she was to teach at Rose's Rescue, the school established by the sheriff's wife for women of all ages escaping life in the cribs.

After the list of gifts, Catherine's letter detailed the twins' graduation. Clara graduated at the top of the class, of course. Catherine didn't mention her marks, only that she received her diploma. Then she launched into a solid two pages of details of parties following graduation.

There wouldn't be such parties as his wife—a fact Catherine had yet to grasp. Would she be content with his lifestyle? Most women in Hiramsville only wore bustles on Sunday. He hadn't seen a single woman in an evening gown since he left Austin, even at the Hiramsville Theater and Opera.

Using a different ink, her letter continued, her letters rushed and botched with ink dots.

> Lewis, I don't know what I should do. Clara confided in me … she has no intention of coming to Hiramsville. She's arranged an elopement with Bernard. I don't understand. She didn't like him that much. I'm sure she only did it to spite me. Since I am older, I've always told her I should marry first. Her plan is to leave with me, then meet him at New York when we transfer trains. I fear for her. She has given me no reason for her decision. However, I have noticed that her clothes are tighter than they were a few months ago. Is it wicked for me to wonder if she is in the family way? A child is the only reason I can think of for her to act so rashly. My parents will cut her off completely if that is the truth of the matter. I cannot stand the stain of losing a sister in such a way.
>
> Please tell no one of my fears. I hope this is all an elaborate joke, like those we used to play on you.

In disbelief, Lewis reread the paragraphs again, and again. Clara would never give herself to a man outside of wedlock. If she was with child, it would be because someone stole her innocence. He'd learned much about judging a woman for that from Emily, Mrs. Reese, and the women at Rose's Rescue.

Circumstances beyond their control forced many women to work in the brothels and cribs. Poor Clara. He could only hope that Bernard was a better man than Catherine believed he was. She'd written of the man courting Clara since before Christmas, although there was no particular attachment that he'd discerned from the letters.

If only he'd asked if the woman he was proposing to was indeed Clara. Or even said Clara's name during the proposal. Then he could have laughed off his mistake and married the twin he favored. He'd hoped that with both of the sisters in Hiramsville that there could be some intervention before the wedding. He needed a miracle not unlike the lamb that saved Isaac from Abraham's sacrifice, where the sisters would realize his mistake and allow him to correct it since their families and friends were not around to witness.

Catherine was not a good fit for him or the ministry. While friendly, she lacked the expected depth of personality. Over the past year, she'd written more about parties, ribbons, and such frivolities than she had her thoughts or feelings. Yet if he didn't wed soon, he would be in danger of losing his post and the congregation he had grown to love.

Lewis knelt next to his desk and prayed more fervently than he had in some months. He prayed that Catherine's suspicions of a child were unfounded. He prayed for Clara's happiness. Finally, he prayed for a miracle that he and Catherine could have a happy life together and that his new wife would never learn of his mistake or how deeply he cared for her twin, an understanding that he'd been slow to recognize. Too slow. When Clara had stopped writing postscripts on Catherine's letters, he'd felt a loss which had only grown.

He prayed that, somehow, he would understand it was God's will that he marry Catherine. It had to be for such a Biblical switch to be made.

Then he prayed again for Clara.

The shadow of the tree outside of his bedroom window moved along the wall and the room dimmed. Still he prayed, and prayed, and prayed until he had no words left and the sleeves of his shirt were damp with tears.

Food had no appeal to him. Lewis climbed into bed with a prayer on his lips. His last conscious thought was of Clara.

Clara's concern grew as Catherine paled with each jolt of the train. "What can I do for you?"

"Help me to the ladies' retiring room. I'm going to—" Catherine held her handkerchief to her mouth.

Other than holding Catherine's elbow, there was little assistance Clara could give in the Pullman car. Clara waited outside the door for her sister to emerge. They'd traveled by train many times, and Catherine had never become ill before. Well, other than their trip home from college in June, but the car had smelled of fish, and most everyone was ill.

The train slowed for a stop at the next station. From experience, Clara knew there would not be enough time to disembark and take a turn in the fresh air. Catherine emerged from the retiring room only slightly less pale.

"Should we have them remove our trunks and return to Boston? We can travel when you are well."

Catherine turned up the aisle. "No, I'll be able to make it to New York."

Clara sat next to her sister. "But New York is only where we change trains."

"I am staying in New York."

"What do you mean?"

"Bernard lives there. We are eloping to Niagara Falls. Then we will live at his parents' home while he builds ours. Fifth Avenue or Long Island, he wasn't sure which."

"You are eloping with my Bernard?" The idea was ludicrous.

"*Your* Bernard?" Catherine's laugh held an edge to it. "You wouldn't even kiss him. He never wrote to you. He was never yours."

An unfortunate slip. "What about Lewis?"

"You are going to marry him."

"I can't. He proposed to you."

"Silly goose. Haven't you realized he only proposed to me because he thought I was you? At the Independence Day picnic, he hardly paid me any attention. It was all you and *sprechen sie Deutsch*. I overheard Mrs. Staples telling mother that he only had a few more days to find a bride, as his superiors wouldn't give him his own church unless he was at least engaged. When I saw him coming over dressed to the nines, I knew he was going to propose. I rushed downstairs, sent the butler on an errand, and removed my jewelry. I thought he would realize his mistake before he finished. Honestly, I only meant it as a joke. But he never called it off. I am not going to live my life in some town with packed dirt roads, quilting for charity."

The bandage Clara kept around her heart all these months tore and her heart bled anew. She fought back tears. "Why didn't you call it off?"

"How could I? You'd seen me kiss him. I couldn't admit what I'd done to Father. He would have made me marry Lewis anyway."

"I only saw him kneeling next to you. I didn't see the kiss." Lewis's face had been bright red with embarrassment, so she'd assumed.

Catherine flicked her hand. "Oh, fiddlesticks. I'd thought you'd seen us. Then Mother came in, and she was gushing. Father was annoyed Lewis hadn't asked permission, and everyone was talking. I was trapped. Why would I want to marry him? Even his letters are dull. Does he think I care what some German guy said about the Gospel of Luke?"

Clara closed her eyes to keep her tears inside. "Why didn't you tell me?"

"And suffer the embarrassment of a failed engagement? Never. I hoped Lewis would admit his mistake. Instead, he told me some drivel about it being God's will. But I've solved it. You are going to Texas and will pretend to be me. You can marry Lewis and everything will be as it should."

"I can't pretend to be you for the rest of my life."

"He'll figure it out eventually, like he always did when we switched places."

"But what of you and why Bernard?" Bernard was the reason she knew she didn't want to be a society wife. He'd only cared for her beauty.

Catherine laughed again. "Oh, my poor, naïve sister. When you altered my graduation dress, or helped me tie my corset strings, did you not wonder why I'd suddenly gained weight when I wasn't eating pounds of sweets? Did it not occur to you that I haven't had a monthly since you had that cold and I went sleigh riding with Bernard anyway?"

"What are you saying?" Clara's ears must be betraying her. Catherine had gained weight, like so many others. All of them had consumed so much chocolate, it was natural. Catherine had ceased accompanying her on walks. The matron stressed the importance of exercise for a woman's figure. Yet, Catherine was alluding to the unthinkable.

"I am in the family way. I expect to be a mother in October. It is Bernard's."

"But? How? When? I don't understand. You can't graduate if you are unchaste." Clara struggled to remain calm so as to not draw the attention of other passengers. Never had a nightmare caused fear and unbelief to course through her as did her sister's revelation.

"Only if they don't know about it, and no one did. Not even you."

"Why?" If she could only understand maybe this could be solved.

"Because once you get used to a man's attentions, there is nothing as thrilling as the feeling of being passionately loved. It is even more exciting than the time we went two whole days with no one realizing we'd traded places." Catherine frowned. "As I remember, Lewis ruined that too."

"That is not love. It's lust." Clara whispered the words, conscious that others might hear.

"They only say that because they have never experienced making love under a flowering cherry tree or hiding in a cloakroom..."

Clara held up her hand. "Stop. No more details."

"You will learn soon enough. It isn't nearly as technical as described in the home nursing class."

Again Catherine's laugh set Clara on edge. Never had Clara been subject to something so inappropriate.

If Clara was younger, she'd have covered her ears to avoid hearing her sister's words. "So you are leaving me to travel to Texas on my own?"

"Yes."

"But I can just return to Boston and tell our parents and the Staples." Clara could wire her friend Emily and tell her she would be a week or so late and hire a traveling companion.

"No, you can't. You dropped a goodbye note that will be delivered tomorrow morning. It starts 'Dear Mother and Father, By the time you read this I will be Mrs. Clara Fairlane.' I ignored the convention of Mrs. Bernard Fairlane to not confuse anyone. Would you like me to continue?"

"What about my job and Lewis?"

"Oh, I took care of that. I sent Lewis a letter saying that you had a plan to elope, and I feared you might be in the family way. Any feelings he may still have for you will transfer to me and guarantee he goes ahead with the marriage as soon as possible. By the time he figures out what happened, the deed will be done. See?"

"I don't see at all. I don't understand why you lied, and why you want me to lie and not just any lie... You want me to live it." One that ruined her reputation and her life. What had changed her sister in so little time? Was it Bernard's influence?

"You've always been such a baby. I did it because I wanted to. Remember the pranks we played?"

"This is not a harmless prank. Mother and Father will think I am some loose woman. You betrayed Lewis, and then there's me." Clara's voice broke and she cleared her throat to force a strength she didn't feel. "Don't you love me at all?"

"I do, but sometimes you are so . . . so . . . I don't know the word—correct? Everything you do is so well thought out and executed. Even when we were little, you were always neat and tidy, prim and proper. Mother was always saying, 'Be more like Clara.' Well, I am tired of trying to be angelically good."

"They told me to be more like you." *Talk more, be more friendly, don't read so much. You're too timid.* All the phrases she'd heard growing up.

"And now you can be me. Ironic isn't it? Both trying to be like the other? I suppose that is why I insisted we switch places so often."

"You used to say you liked the thrill from tricking people." A thrill that Clara had never understood.

"You were always worried about being caught. No one will be able to this time."

"I can't do this. I am not you. I am me." Clara's heart raced as panic set in. Catherine was not teasing or telling a story.

"But you have to. If you don't, Lewis will lose his church. His superiors only made him a full pastor because he was getting married after that other guy got sick. We both listened to him whine to Clifford when he was at Harvard about how much he didn't think finance or law was for him. He's been so pleasant these last summers while being at the seminary— even if he became a bore quoting scriptures. You wouldn't condemn him to a life balancing books, would you?"

Catherine was right. Lewis had hated his time at Harvard. Especially his math classes. "Lewis's insights are not boring. Of course, I don't want him to hold a job he doesn't enjoy for his entire life. Why can't I just marry him as me—Clara?"

"Everyone in Texas knows he is marrying Catherine. How embarrassing for him if he marries a Clara instead? And what of his superiors? If they find out he only continued his engagement to the wrong sister so he could keep his position, he will lose all their respect. You would ruin the man you love."

"What?" Clara had never spoken her feelings for him out loud. Even when they'd been younger, she'd admired her brother's friend as her own.

"*Love,*" Catherine insisted. "You have been over the moon for him for years. I see the way your eyes light up when he speaks to you, and you are as bad as a puppy dog begging for a bone when I receive a letter from him. Even a few boring sentences bring a smile to your face."

"But he has come to love you." He must have. Otherwise, why would he have proposed? Clara stared at her sister, unable to find more words. Her best friend, her confidante, the person she would do anything for was betraying her for what? The thrill of changing places? Because she'd yielded to the lusts of the flesh they'd so often been warned about?

Catherine stood. "I need to go to the retiring room again."

Clara watched out the window as they sped by trees and buildings. They would be in New York near sunset. Only a few hours to decide.

The hardest problem was figuring out when Catherine had been lying and where she told the truth. The proposal. Could Lewis have mixed them up? Not if they'd been together, but they'd been apart at the time. Catherine had even fooled their mother that way before. Lewis wouldn't have backed out of the engagement after the announcement. One of their last conversations had been discussing when something was God's inspiration and not man's imagination. Was it possible that Lewis had taken Catherine's deception as divine intervention? From the portions of the letters Catherine had read to her, Clara knew he was trying to get to know her sister on a more intimate level and build a godly relationship.

As far as her sister being with child, it was true she'd gained weight lately with both her waist and bosom growing larger. The seamstress had been quite put out at the last wedding gown fitting. Had Catherine known what she was doing with Bernard? After some of the basic medical sessions they'd had at Bradford, it would have been difficult not to know how a child was conceived. Since Bernard didn't force a kiss with her when she'd refused, it was likely he hadn't forced more with her sister. It would have been Catherine's choice. Her sister spoke as if there had been multiple liaisons.

Clara shuddered, unable to believe the truth.

Catherine returned.

"How is this supposed to work?" asked Clara.

Her twin smiled. "I knew you would go through with it. That is why I repacked some of our trunks…"

As Clara listened to the plan, an unnamed horror grew. If her sister put as much time into her schoolwork as she had this scheme, she may have graduated with honors as well.

⟢◆⟣

God spoke to some men through dreams. Peter, Paul, and Isaiah were all proof of that. There was nothing saying that God spoke to normal men that way. Still, the dream that woke Lewis in the darkest hours of the night seemed more than a normal dream. Clara and Catherine were in it. He knew which one was who because they wore their hair bows. But then Catherine kept switching them faster and faster until he lost track of who was who. A voice told him to close his eyes and listen. Their voices. The way they spoke was different. Then he'd heard Clara calling for help. He'd tried to find her, only his eyes wouldn't open.

Once he got his breathing returned to normal, he lay back down and willed sleep to come. For a half hour, he tossed and turned. His concern for Clara grew with each passing tick of the clock.

Still in his nightshirt, he went to his office and lit a lamp. Moving a stack of books aside, he started a letter.

July 6, 1880

My dear Clara,

I don't know where to send this. Your sister has informed me of your plans, and my heart is heavy. I could have prevented this if I'd only had the courage to speak up.

Last July, I came to propose to you. I do not understand how I didn't perceive it was Catherine who led me into the parlor. If I had only said your dear name once, there would have been no confusion that she was not the object of my proposal. Once she'd accepted, I felt committed. I have tried in vain these months to get to know your sister beyond the teasing she has shown me since our childhood.

I have come to the conclusion that your sister and I will know no felicity in our union. We will constantly be at odds in our thoughts, and how can I counsel others if I am resentful?

I wish I could go back and change what happened a year ago. I should have owned the mistake and let Catherine pout and stomp about as I begged for your understanding.

I do not know what circumstances have brought you to this elopement; I cannot help but think he coerced you in some way, just as Catherine would do when you were young. How often did she leave you in precarious situations, up trees or drenched in mud, and you never complained?

I do not know how to make this right. However, I know I will only compound the wrong by marrying Catherine.

My superiors may demote me for breaking the engagement. Know that it is not your fault. Perhaps this is my Jonah moment, but I have known no peace of mind or heart this past year. I cannot say with certainty that God will approve, but I must find happiness.

If you should ever need me, I will be here.

Always yours,

Lewis

He took out a second paper and dated it.

Catherine,

I must right the wrongs that I have committed.

The day I proposed, I thought I was proposing to Clara. I do not have a good excuse for why I have waited until Clara is beyond all reach to rectify the situation. I cannot marry you.

You would, no doubt, find joy in the social aspects of the job of being a minister's wife, leading the benevolent society and such, but as my wife, you would never be happy. When there was enough money for new clothes, they would not be fashionable. There wouldn't be parties and gossip as your letters show you still enjoy.

If you want to take your sister's position with Emily, you may. Otherwise, I implore you to take the first train home. I have some small funds saved up that I hope will be enough for the journey.

I wish you well, my friend.

Be happy.

Lewis

He did not know where to send Clara's letter, and for Catherine's, he would only give it to her if he could not find courage to say the same to her upon her arrival. He still would need to write to his superiors. Such a letter was better composed after Catherine made her choice to work or to leave.

Lewis left the letters on his desk and returned to his room for whatever rest he could find.

Mr. Rooster, however, saw no reason that Lewis should sleep at all.

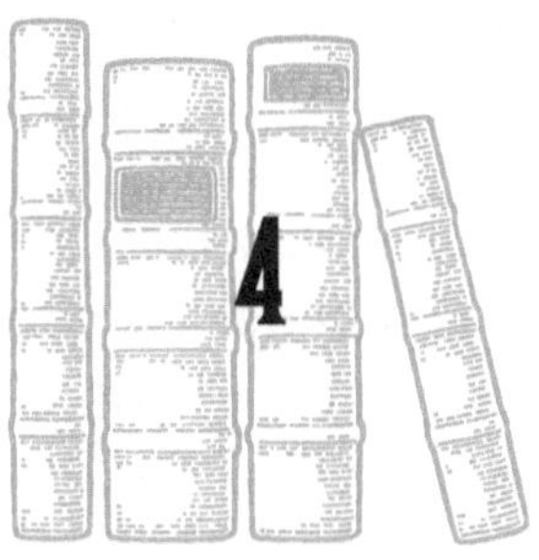

lara stood in front of the smudged mirror in the ladies' lounge of the Fort Worth train station. She wore the necklace Catherine had given her in New York before she'd disappeared into the sea of people, followed by a porter and her trunks. Bernard was not to be seen, which was both a relief and a worry. Now that she'd had days alone on the train to think about it, she saw how often Bernard had found reasons to be with Catherine, and vice versa. So many times, he'd insisted that Catherine not be stuck at the dorm simply because she was engaged. Or the times Catherine had begged to be part of an outing.

At one of the longer train stops, Clara found a skein of soft yellow yarn and started a crochet blanket for the niece or nephew that would arrive before winter. Hopefully, she would know where to send it and be able to seek Catherine's friendship once again.

It was much harder to forgive her sister's betrayal this time than it had been for eating the last of the cook's chocolate creams that everyone knew was for Clara, or any one of the other daily slights she'd endured most of her life. Why couldn't Catherine admit she'd been playing one of her tricks that day a year ago? Even if she had kissed Lewis. Of course, there would have been some embarrassment and anger, but it would have been kept within the family. Then, if Lewis had really wanted to propose to her and not to Catherine, he could have. Now she would never know what Lewis had been thinking. Her sister was correct on that point. No matter who he married, he would honor his vows. And perhaps, like the novel she'd read that was about an arranged marriage, he would come to love her in time.

Even better, he would realize who she was before the marriage and want to wed her, because she was Clara. If her sister was correct, he had some feelings for her. Their friendship was still better than only being adored for one's hairstyle or clothing.

Despite her worries about completing the trip alone, none of the scenarios of her mother's dime novels befell her. Clara found a delightful traveling companion in a widow who was on the same train as far as Fort Worth. As long as she was willing to take the upper berth, Clara had not had to share a bed each night. She was so used to sharing with Catherine, that sleeping with a stranger would have been very difficult. That thought led to one about sharing a bed with Lewis, which she quickly dismissed. If he hadn't discovered by their wedding night that he married a deceiver, he'd know then. Unlike her sister, she'd never kissed a man and wasn't at all sure how it should be done.

The clock on the wall announced fifteen minutes until her train. Clara settled her sister's red-ribboned hat on her head and secured it with a long hatpin. With the hat on, she resembled Catherine more. Clara squared her shoulders and left the lounge. She located her trunks and made sure they were on the westbound train before boarding to find a seat among the wooden benches.

There were few enough people in the car that she was not forced to share the wooden bench seat.

A man wearing a cowboy hat watched her every move. Like other men she'd seen, he wore a gun belt. What if he was an outlaw? Or had nefarious plans for her, now that she was unchaperoned?

Avoiding his eye, Clara looked out the window and played with the pendant of the necklace. The windows cast a faint reflection of her looking so much like Catherine, she thought she saw her sister rather than herself. The necklace was the one Lewis had given Catherine at the small farewell party-turned engagement party the night before he'd left. Clara dropped her hand, aware that not only was she bringing attention to the gold chain and pendant, but that Catherine never played with her jewelry. The ruse would fail. Lewis wouldn't believe she was Catherine for even ten minutes.

Perhaps it was best if she didn't pretend at all.

Catherine's warnings sounded in Clara's head. If the church leadership realized that he married someone else, the consequences could be many. Her only choice was to fool him. But he would recognize her, wouldn't he? He must. If Lewis didn't recognize her, then maybe Catherine was wrong, and he'd never thought of her as a potential bride. All her life she'd been confused with her sister. She wanted a husband who never would think her to be Catherine or wonder if twins were interchangeable.

The train rattled along the tracks. Maybe she shouldn't get off when she got to Hiramsville. She could go to the next town and find a hotel, write a letter to Lewis, and catch the first train that would take her home. The ten double eagles were safe in the lining of her corset. In time, she could convince her mother the letter was one of Catherine's ruses.

The conductor walked down the aisle checking tickets. He paused at hers. "Hiramsville is the next stop. You must be the new preacher's bride. Welcome to Texas, ma'am."

Unable to speak, Clara nodded. There would be no missing her stop now. The cowboy looked her way again. Clara turned away and fought off the fear threatening to overrule her good senses. She could do this.

In time, Lewis would forgive her. After all, she was saving his job and reputation.

⊰◈⊱

Lewis paced the length of the Hiramsville station and prayed. In the distance, a train whistled. Right on time. A few other people milled about the station. Some, like the mercantile owner, had a reason to be here, others were there to watch him.

The sheriff, TJ, and his wife, Emily, stood in the shade of the station, likely there to greet Clara, who'd taken a teaching position at Rose's Rescue. How would they react when they realized their new teacher wasn't coming? Despite Catherine's request, he should have told them their new teacher wouldn't arrive. Emily had recruited from her friends at Bradford College hopeful that two would take jobs. Only Clara applied, others had been put off by Emily's harrowing experience last summer.

The train pulled to a stop, sending a burst of steam momentarily obliterating his view. The first man off the train looked familiar but was not part of his flock. A cowboy, perhaps. The sheriff welcomed the man with a handshake and a hug. Ah. The ranger with the initial name like his brother the sheriff. A family climbed down next. Finally, Catherine appeared. Her red hat sat jauntily on her head. Lewis rushed forward to help her with her valise and the hatbox she carried.

She looked at him and something flashed in her eyes that he couldn't read. She straightened her stance and lifted her chin. She'd changed. Maybe it was the fatigue of the trip.

The pendant. Of all her jewelry, she'd chosen to wear his engagement gift. Surprising, since she'd complained it didn't suit her normal attire. Conversation would have to wait until they could be in private. "Allow me to take your things."

"Thank you." Her voice. Could it be Clara? He looked again, unsure. If only one of them had a visible scar. Clara had a long one below her knee from a fall when the gate had broken as she'd swung on it. But that wasn't a place he could ask to look, even in private. Lewis offered his elbow. "Allow me to escort you to the wagon I borrowed. Your trunks won't fit in a buggy."

She answered with a nod. Again, a very Clara way of communicating—not even a complaint about the mode of transportation. The buggy was far from new, and he worried what Catherine might say of it.

Lewis fought to keep his face passive. The clothing said Catherine, the necklace said Catherine, and the letter had said Catherine. The mannerisms said Clara.

Catherine would not have missed the opportunity to kiss him the moment she stepped off the train, or, at the very least, shout his name and throw herself into his arms for all to see. She loved an audience.

Emily, TJ, and the ranger met them at the side of the wagon.

"Catherine, I love your hat. Where is Clara?" asked Emily.

The hand on his arm tightened. "She was unable to come."

Emily tilted her head. "Catherine, are you well?"

The woman on his arm fanned her face. "Only tired. I wasn't expecting the heat."

"I remember my trip out here last year. I was so happy to be off the train—until I landed in jail." Emily looked up at her husband, teasing evident in her eyes. "Word to the wise, it is much warmer in the jail cells."

TJ wrapped his arm around Emily's waist. "Best arrest I ever made."

"Oh, this is my husband TJ and his brother GW. GW is a Texas Ranger, although at the moment, he looks a bit more like an outlaw."

The ranger tipped his hat in greeting before glaring at his brother. "If you two make lovey eyes at the station, I'll arrest you for public indecency."

Catherine didn't attempt to outdo the couple's loving looks. Instead, she looked anywhere but at Lewis's face.

"Welcome to town, ma'am." TJ nodded at the trunks sitting next to the boxcar. "Preacher, can we help you with her trunks?"

"If you would, please."

Emily kissed her husband's cheek before letting him go. The ranger followed them to the trunks.

TJ stood with his back to the ladies and grabbed a handle of the larger trunk. "Preacher, my wife just told me that woman is Clara. What is going on?"

"I was coming to that conclusion myself. I am still not sure which twin it is—Clara pretending to be Catherine, or Catherine acting like Clara. They've fooled me before." Lewis grabbed the other end of the trunk while GW hoisted the smaller one onto his shoulder.

"How are you going to figure it out?"

"Darned if I know. I haven't seen either of them for a year." Neither man reacted to the minor expletive which slipped out before Lewis thought through the sentence.

When they returned to the wagon, Emily and whichever twin exchanged a hug.

Emily stepped back. "When you are rested, we must get together and chat. I want to hear about what everyone is doing."

Lewis helped his fiancée up onto the wagon seat. Still, she made no move to embrace him.

He rounded the wagon and climbed up. Miss Taylor looked back at the trunks, her eyebrows furrowed. Her left hand clasped the pendant at her throat.

"Is something wrong?"

"I was sure I only had two trunks. All three have my initials on them."

"Perhaps Clara left one when she eloped."

The woman coughed and reddened. "Of course, that must be the answer."

A curious development, to be sure.

An idea came to him. There was one way he could tell. He turned down the road by the river and pulled the wagon to a stop under a copse of trees that provided both shade and a bit of privacy.

<hr>

Lewis stopped the wagon and turned to stare at her.

Had he already guessed? Clara clutched her purse tighter. She looked around, seeing no one else. "Is something wrong?"

Lewis slid closer on the wagon bench. "Not particularly."

Her pulse raced. Out of nervousness or his nearness, she wasn't sure. "Why did you stop?"

He lifted his hand to her face. His fingers slid along her jaw, gently turning her to face him eye to eye.

His gaze was so intense, she closed her eyes to prevent him from looking too deeply. There was something in his touch that was causing her to tingle.

He knew.

He had to know. Her exit from the train had given her away. Catherine would have rushed to him. She'd planned to, until she saw him standing there confident in his clerical collar, more handsome than he'd been a year ago.

"Darling?"

Her eyes opened to his call. What would Catherine do?

He leaned closer. His voice rumbled low. "We didn't have a proper greeting."

"Oh." No! He wanted to kiss her. What was she supposed to do? Close her eyes? Leave them open? Were her lips meant to move or brush each other. Catherine would know, she'd kissed several men. His face descended. She pinched her eyes shut, so he wouldn't see her surprise or uncertainty. His index finger lifted her chin and his lips met hers. The brief contact was no more than a brush. She survived her first kiss. His hand moved to the side of her face. Again, his lips caressed hers. The shock of this second touch caused her to gasp.

Lewis moved closer to her, pressing his lips more firmly against hers. His hand found her waist and held her in place. Clara's brain ceased to function and something inside her chest awoke as her lips instinctively responded to his. Her hand moved up and felt the warmth radiating off his shirt, or was it just the sensation of the fire within her?

He broke the kiss, leaving a few inches between their faces but still holding on to her waist. "Welcome to Hiramsville. I'm very glad you are here."

Lewis dropped his hand and picked up the reins, urging the horses forward.

Clara looked away. Part of her wanted to cry. He hadn't recognized her.

Her first kiss. One to match every story she'd ever heard, and it wasn't even meant for her. She pinched her eyes closed. Pain sliced through her. If only she could tell him he was wrong, and then slap his face for taking such liberties with his kiss. Perhaps it would stop the pain.

He hadn't meant it for her.

The wagon wheel hit a bump. She tightened her grip on the seat. With it, she tightened her resolve. She couldn't confess yet. It would ruin him. Clara would not be responsible for Lewis losing his place and the job he loved. Perhaps one day, after he forgave her, there would be another kiss like that, one intended specifically for her.

They turned a corner and stopped in front of a grand house that rivaled those in Brookline. Even the white gingerbread work reminded her of home. Lewis helped her down and led her to the front door, which stood open behind a wire screen. As they approached, the screen door opened.

A girl of about sixteen or maybe younger smiled and yelled. "Mrs. Reese, she's here!"

The girl stepped out onto the porch that circled the house. "You are as pretty as the preacher said. I thought he was exaggerating."

A woman, her hair touched with gray, appeared behind the girl. "Becky, please stop gawking." She turned her attention to Clara. "Welcome. Come on in. I'm Mrs. Reese."

"Nice to meet you." Clara tilted her head as her mother had taught her.

"Where is your sister?" asked Mrs. Reese.

"There was a last-moment change of plans. I'm afraid she won't be coming." It wasn't a lie exactly. Still, Clara hated herself for saying it.

"Reverend, if you will get her things, I'll have Nellie serve lemonade and sandwiches."

Lewis touched her elbow. "Which trunk do you need?"

Clara tried to hide her shock at his touch. It took a moment for words to form. Clothes and books she needed were packed in both trunks. He'd need help lifting the large one up the stairs. "The small one, please."

Lewis bounded off the porch.

Mrs. Reese led Clara into the parlor. "I imagine you are torn between wanting to visit with your beloved and wishing for a cool bath."

Clara touched her hair. "I feel as though I am carting about a bucket of ash in my hair alone."

"And you would be more comfortable conversing with your intended after you are washed. I understand. I'll endeavor to send him away as quickly as possible. Becky can help wash your hair, if you wish."

"That sounds divine." Clara sat on the far end of the davenport where Mrs. Reese indicated she should. The widow, judging from her deep gray gown, sat in a wingback chair.

Another girl about Becky's size entered the room carrying a silver tray with three glass tumblers in one hand and a pitcher of lemonade with ice in the other. She set both down on the table. Clara forced a smile. Scars marred the young woman's face. Never had she seen such a terrifying visage. Only her mother's deportment lessons kept Clara from gasping.

"It's alright if you look, Miss. Most people need to the first time they meet me. I'm Nellie. I run the kitchen at Rose's Rescue. Mrs. Reese thought it best if I met you and your sister here. The last teacher had no warning…"

"Emily wrote you were the best cook in the county, unless it came to peach pie." Clara tapped her chin, trying to remember the name of the woman who ran the hotel.

"Miss Emily is too kind. Hannah cooks heaps better than me, as does Thelma, who usually cooks for Mrs. Reese. Where's your sister?"

Clara startled at the question. Lewis had known to only expect one of them. "She had a change of plans…"

"Oh." Nellie frowned. "Miss Emily said your sister would be the one to teach us elocution. I want to learn how to look everyone in the eye when I talk with them. I don't need to be ashamed because my ma done poured lye on me." The girl readied three glasses of the lemonade and handed one to Clara.

"You are doing an excellent job of it without lessons. However, if you'd like, I can teach you." It was the least Clara could do, having ruined this girl's hopes of lessons.

"You'll be busy being married to the preacher and all."

"I am sure I can make some time."

Lewis entered the parlor. "Becky had me put the trunk in your room. I also took up your hatbox and the valise."

"Thank you." Clara nodded her head, mostly to not need to make eye contact. At any moment, Lewis could learn his error and realize who he'd kissed.

He lowered himself onto the davenport next to Clara. She clutched her drink with both hands. Any excuse not to touch him again. Only if she didn't, he would figure it out sooner. The wedding was days away. It wasn't supposed to be this difficult to pretend to be Catherine. Her sister wouldn't be afraid to touch or kiss him.

Mrs. Reese set her tumbler back on the tray. "Reverend, your bride-to-be is too modest to ask, however, she would love to clean up after her days on the train. Perhaps you could join us for a late breakfast around ten tomorrow. Give her some time to rest as well."

Lewis hopped up. "Oh my darling, I hadn't realized. I should have thought. Why didn't you say something?"

Why indeed? Catherine would have let her desires be known at the station. "I didn't want to rush you off."

"Understandable. We can catch up tomorrow. My sermon is prepared, so I have all of Saturday at my disposal." Lewis reached for her hand.

Unsure what to do, Clara stood.

He pressed his lips to the back of her still-gloved fingers. At least she'd remembered to leave them on. Catherine never bit at her nails. She must remember to keep them hidden from him.

"I'll see myself out."

At the screen door, she stood as if in a haze and watched him go. It was like being trapped in a dream where everything was wrong but she couldn't change anything. It would not surprise her at all if she were able to fly about the room next.

"Oh, you poor thing, you are stretched to the limit. Come, I'll show you to the bathroom."

Clara followed Mrs. Reese to the back of the house. Bath or not, she needed the time alone to figure out how to survive the next several days.

The sheriff's office below the jail was empty. The door to the residence stood open, and voices came from the parlor. Lewis tapped on the door frame.

Emily looked up from the pitcher she was pouring. "Reverend, back so soon?"

Lewis stepped into the room, conscious that with GW there, he likely had interrupted a family reunion, but he needed answers. "How did you know she was Clara?"

TJ pointed to the empty chair as a way of invitation.

Emily waited for Lewis to sit. "For the first few minutes, I didn't. The red hat fooled me, but once she was close enough to see her eyes, I knew. I don't understand. Where is Catherine, and why is Clara pretending to be her?"

"I don't understand either. Clara never corrected me or Mrs. Reese." The stiff, now unnecessary, letters to the sisters poked him through his pocket. Lewis adjusted his jacket.

"But you weren't expecting two people. You didn't look around for the other twin." The Texas Ranger had a keen sense of observation.

Lewis looked apologetically at Emily. "I received a letter on Monday saying only Catherine was coming. I should have told you, but I didn't know how to without ruining Clara's reputation since Catherine claimed she'd eloped. Now I have no idea what is going on, and I am positive the woman who got off the train is Clara."

"Do you think it is something criminal?" asked TJ.

"No. What could be criminal about twins switching places?" asked Lewis.

"It all depends on what name she puts on the wedding license," drawled GW. "It is a crime to misidentify yourself."

"You won't arrest her, will you?"

"No." The brothers answered in unison.

TJ continued, "Unless you ask us to."

Emily cleared her throat. "From experience, I can tell you that arresting your bride isn't a good idea. Those cells upstairs are terribly uncomfortable in the summer."

TJ turned to his wife and kissed her cheek. "I'd do it again, if it meant saving you."

"I will not ask you to arrest Clara, even if she is pretending to be Catherine. But why? I thought I understood God's will for me."

"What do you mean?" asked Emily.

"Maybe if you tell us some more, we can figure it out." The ranger took a long sip of his drink.

"I grew up next to the Taylors. Clifford, their older brother, was my best friend. The girls were always about. As I neared the end of my time at the seminary, the woman I hoped to marry chose someone else. Our sect has had some problems in the past with bachelor preachers and the congregations. Now, the leadership encourages—more like demands—us to be married or at least engaged before taking our posts. I didn't have many prospects. At graduation, I was told I needed to be engaged by the time I took up my first posting. I returned to my parents' home and pondered and prayed over who God wanted me to marry. One afternoon, I looked out of the window and saw the twins and knew that I had found my answer. I should marry one of them. Again I pondered. Catherine is able to make friends with everyone and is always so cheerful. She would make a good minister's wife. On the other hand, Clara is quiet and extremely kind. Her conversations are always —" Lewis paused for a breath and to find the right word. "Her conversation was always what I needed: thought provoking. On Independence Day, a week before I was to leave, we had the most amiable conversation in German, of all things. We had always gotten on well considering our different ages. Although she is nearly five years my junior, I've always been drawn to her—something I never fully admitted, even to myself, as her brother would have beaten me soundly if he knew I had any feelings for his younger sister. That night, I decided I would propose to Clara."

Emily held up her hand to stop the narrative. "Did you ever call on either of them?"

"No. Why should I? I've known them since childhood. There was nothing to learn about them I didn't know. Besides, if I called on one and realized I should marry the other, I would have ruined my chance. Calling on one sister then the other isn't done."

"Continue." Emily's tone was as expressionless as her face.

"So, the next evening, I went to the Taylor's intent on proposing to Clara—only I mistook Catherine for Clara. Not to be indelicate, but we sealed the proposal with a kiss. I knew the second she kissed me, I'd made a mistake. I didn't expect Clara to be so forward. Then everything happened so fast. Clara came in, and left, then her parents arrived. I hadn't spoken with her father…"

This time it was TJ who stopped the story. "So, you're saying you proposed to the sister you didn't want to marry and didn't correct it?"

"I'm a minister. I cannot create contention."

"Isn't that what you are supposed to do? Call us to repentance? Contend with us to be better?" asked Emily.

Lewis shifted uncomfortably. He had no intention of making Emily upset. "That is sharing the word. Not what I do personally."

"So, you stayed engaged to Catherine to not create contention?" Emily's voice rose.

"Yes. I could not go back on my word. I assumed the mix up must be God's will and I had gotten things wrong. Much like Esau and Jacob switched their birthrights."

Emily glared at him as if he was an errant schoolboy. "I've corresponded several times this year with Clara. I don't think she was happy. In fact, I don't think she was happy at the station. Catherine has obviously decided not to come, and no offense, but you haven't seemed as excited as a man should be facing marriage. How can it be God's will to make three people unhappy?"

Lewis held his hands up to stop Emily's ranting. "Now, calm down."

"I am calm. You just told us you proposed to a logical choice, to a woman you hadn't courted, realized you proposed to the wrong woman, and did nothing about it. Preacher, I've never said anything like this to a man of the cloth—" she pointed a finger at him. "—but you are a coward."

Lewis opened his mouth. No words came.

TJ spit part of his drink back in his cup.

Emily continued as if no one had reacted to her insult. "We can't all wait around for God to tell us what to do. What if I had done that a year ago? I prayed to get out of Belle's and those caves, but then I did all I could to save myself. If

I hadn't taken action and the worst had happened, should I have just said, 'It's God's will that I be prostituted or murdered?'"

"Of course not. He doesn't want anyone murdered. That is why he gave us commandments."

"Yet murders and terrible things happen to good people. That is why TJ and GW work so hard."

TJ took Emily's hand in his.

She looked at her husband and blinked. "What was my point?"

"You were telling the preacher he was a coward." The sheriff's voice was low and soothing.

"Yes, he is, and I stand by it. You don't deserve Clara or Catherine."

Lewis offered his only defense. "But I still want Clara. I always did."

"Why didn't you do something about it a year ago?" asked Emily.

Lewis stared at his empty hands. "I didn't know how to without hurting someone. You're correct; I acted cowardly."

"So, who do you want to marry?" asked TJ.

"Clara?" Lewis's voice wavered.

Emily glared at him.

"Clara." He answered more firmly.

"Why?" asked Emily.

"She'd be a good minister's wife."

Emily stood and crossed the room, muttering something under her breath. When she turned to face Lewis, her face was calm. "You never said how you figured out she was Clara."

"Easy. I kissed her."

"And?" Emily took a step forward.

"Unlike Catherine, she wasn't practiced." Lewis shrugged a shoulder.

Emily threw up her hands. "Reverend, I take back what I said earlier. You are not a coward. You are the most bone-headed, ignorant, spineless coward I've ever met."

"What?" Lewis couldn't believe the well-mannered sheriff's wife spoke to him that way.

"You heard me. Come next week when Reverend Green comes to conduct your vows and asks if anyone has reason to object, I'll say it again." Emily took her hat off the peg on the wall and set it on her head. "Don't wait up for me. I have a friend with a broken heart to visit." She pointed to GW and TJ. "Whatever you do, don't you dare say it's just women and to ignore me and ruin all the confidence in men you have instilled in me. Y'all might want to impart some wisdom to the good reverend."

None of the men moved until they heard her footfalls on the boardwalk outside.

"Where did I go wrong?" Lewis asked no one in particular.

GW chuckled. "Preacher, even I know better than to tell a woman to calm down."

TJ shook his head. "Reverend, there are only two good reasons to kiss a woman. One is because you love her. Two is to get her to calm down, but she has to think it is because you love her, or you'll be paying for it. But if you kiss her because you love her, but she thinks you are trying to calm her down... well, you better go buy her favorite candy fast."

⟫◆⟪

Even after a pre-bath brushing, the rinse water had a gray tinge to it. How was it possible that sitting on a train for five days could render one so filthy? Clara emptied the tub and refilled it, pleased that the water remained clear.

Feeling clean at last, Clara retired to her room to dry her waist-length hair. Nellie left a plate of cold chicken sandwiches, more than enough for an evening meal.

Slowly working from the ends to her roots, Clara combed out her hair. As she deemed each strand snarl-free, Clara moved it over to the other shoulder, careful not to snag the hair on her chair. She'd already had to reposition herself when she'd sat on it. Catherine had cut her hair to her mid-back a couple of years ago. Perhaps it would be wise to do the same now that there was no one to help her with it each day.

Someone tapped on the door.

"Come in."

Clara expected it to be Nellie or Becky for the tray. It wasn't. Her first reaction was to try to roll her hair up to hide its length.

"Clara, don't bother hiding your hair. I knew it was you at the station." Emily tossed her hat on the bed. "Here, let me comb it for you."

Clara handed over the comb. "How did you know?"

"How could I not know? I lived across the hall from you for a year. What I don't understand is why you are here and why the reverend said you'd eloped."

"And why didn't he realize I wasn't his fiancée?"

"And that." Emily's soft smile put her at ease.

"I don't know where to start."

"Then start where we left off last year. I assume Lewis is the neighbor you've been in love with half of your life."

"Was. I was in love with." The kiss left her with a feeling of loss. Love wasn't supposed to make one feel lonely.

"You have lost all feeling for him?"

"I don't know. Since he proposed to my sister last summer, I've tried to put him out of my mind. I thought I had succeeded…" Clara dropped her eyes. She didn't need to see her own pain in the mirror.

"But?"

"On the train, Catherine was sick, and then she told me this crazy story about how she tricked Lewis into proposing.

Only Lewis never said anything about proposing to the wrong sister. Then she tells me she is sick on the train because she is with child. And she is leaving to elope with Bernard."

"Bernard, as in Bernard Fairlane, who'd been courting you?"

"He took me to events, often with Catherine also, but we never had an understanding. A month before graduation, he told me, while it had been fun, he thought I might make someone else a better wife. Catherine said I should have let him kiss me, but I didn't feel for him like I'd once felt for Lewis. I was relieved to a point. I knew I couldn't spend the rest of my life with Bernard. Now I discover it was never me. He hadn't wanted to court me at all. Just like Lewis, he'd rather have Catherine."

"Is she really in the family way?"

"I believe so. Her clothes don't fit her as well, and she's been ill. I just don't understand how she could have done this. Or that Bernard was using me to see Catherine. I don't know how to feel. How could my sister take the only two men who have ever shown interest in me? Why would neither man care?"

The comb caught in a tangle. "Sorry."

Clara inspected a strand of her hair. "I should cut it off, but I fear it is my one beauty."

"Perhaps just a trim?"

"I could cut off a full foot, and it would still be longer than Catherine's. Not that people use that to tell us apart now that we wear our hair up."

"Better trim it now than after the wedding. TJ gets all bent out of shape when I trim my hair, and I hear other wives say the same about their husbands."

Using her fingers as scissors Clara tested different lengths in the mirror. "I'm afraid that the scissors in my sewing kit are not very sharp."

"Mrs. Reese might have some that we can borrow. It doesn't need to be tonight. You can't be married before next Wednesday anyway."

"Why?" asked Clara.

"That is when the visiting preacher is coming. Didn't the reverend tell you?"

"He may assume I already know. After all, he thinks I am Catherine."

"Are you sure?"

"He must. He kissed me without asking permission or anything. If he thought it was me…" Tears that had been building for days flooded Clara's eyes. It wasn't fair that her first kiss was so perfect, everything she'd ever wondered about and more, except that the man who'd poured so much emotion into the kiss had meant it for another. It hadn't been hers to take, yet she'd accepted it. Guilt added itself to her emotions.

Emily wrapped her arms around Clara and walked with her from the dressing table stool to a small fainting couch near the window where they could sit side by side. Tear after tear fell. Some were for her broken heart which had never gotten over losing Lewis to Catherine. Many were for Catherine. Her sister would be lost to her for some time, if not forever. Bernard wouldn't bring Catherine to Texas. What would Clara go home to? Her parents weren't likely to believe the story against Catherine's letter at least for a while when Clara showed no signs of impending motherhood. It would all be so unsettling for everyone. Keeping her hair meant keeping a part of her. Clara abandoned the plan to cut it off. Though a trim was in order.

"She told everyone I was eloping. I wonder if Bernard even knows who he is marrying. Now for the rest of my life, I have to be her or I will ruin Lewis's ministry as well."

"Why would you ruin his ministry?"

"He told his supervisors he was engaged to Catherine when he took the post. It would look like he was lying if he married someone else, and if he didn't get married, they could remove him."

"I don't see how that's your problem. You can't spend the rest of your life pretending to be someone you aren't just to make others happy."

"But if he loses his post…"

"What if he discovers you are Clara after he marries Catherine and realizes his entire marriage isn't legal?"

Clara sucked in a breath. "Oh, that would be terrible."

"According to TJ and GW, you could end up in jail."

"That would be a scandal. The church leaders would not be happy about that." Every iota of her sister's plan fell apart. It could never work.

"I imagine not. What if your family were ever to visit. What would happen then?"

Clara sat motionless for a moment, running through the outcomes in her mind. Her mother would realize immediately what had happened, as would her brother. Worse yet, what if they were to travel back to Boston? Both families would be shamed at the discovery. "What am I supposed to do?"

"How many 'the truth will set you free' sermons have you attended?"

"More than I can count. But that wasn't what I was thinking. Once the truth comes out, what should I do?"

"You could come work at the Rescue like you planned. And tell the truth about Catherine not coming."

"What about Lewis? He still needs a wife."

"Let me ask you this. Do you love him?"

"I don't know anymore."

"Then maybe you can wait until you know. Better than rushing into something."

Clara gave Emily a tight squeeze. "I am so glad you are here."

ewis spent a sleepless night pondering on the day's events. He'd stayed at the sheriff's as long as he dared, wondering what Emily might say to Clara after such an outburst. The brothers didn't have any sound advice for him either. The ranger claimed he never understood women. TJ seemed either unwilling or unsure to say what he understood about Emily.

He reread Catherine's last letter. Why had she lied about Clara eloping? Did she think he would be easily fooled by the switch? Even when the girls were younger, it had always been Clara, either by a look or an action, who revealed they had switched places. She didn't slide into Catherine's light-hearted gregariousness as easily as her sister could take on Clara's quiet traits.

What if the ruse wasn't about fooling him? What if it was about the Bernard fellow? Catherine's letters often spoke of how dull she found school… Still, it was hard to believe that she might have engaged in fornication. Everything about the situation was troubling.

As he riffled through the old letters, he kept hearing Emily's voice in his head calling him a coward.

Before the last years of seminary, he would have handled the proposal to Catherine differently. He would have admitted his error and begged for Clara's understanding, and asked Clara who she was at the train station, not caring if an argument broke out. He shuffled Catherine's letters back together. One of the postscripts caught his eye. It was in Clara's hand.

> *P. S. Our new theology teacher says that meekness is often seen as a weakness, and has no place in modern times. I maintain that meekness is a strength. However, people often confuse it with being overly agreeable rather than the humility it should be. What are your thoughts?*

As he recalled, he'd tried to answer the question by saying that meekness was often mistaken as a weakness because Christians turned the other cheek. Clara argued that being meek didn't mean you couldn't fight back and dropped the subject. In fact, she hadn't added any postscripts to her sister's letters after that. He'd missed them. They'd been the best part of the weekly letters. Catherine's letters grew more and more mundane with each passing week. It was as if she'd been deliberately trying to bore him.

Perhaps she had been.

Somewhere a cock crowed. Lewis rubbed his eyes. Dawn had yet to lighten the eastern sky; perhaps an hour of sleep would be better than none. Only pausing long enough to extinguish the lantern and put the letters away, Lewis went in search of sleep. Facing the wall, he hoped to hide from the morning light for as long as possible. However, the kiss that had so enraged Emily played in his mind. The first brush of his lips confirmed Clara's identity by her innocence and uncertainty. He hadn't meant to take it further, but he couldn't resist rejoicing that somehow God had put everything to rights. A fire burned inside of him he hadn't anticipated. He wanted more, needed more. He'd never felt such a desire with Catherine's passionate kisses they'd shared in the few days before his departure.

The kiss didn't feel wrong. Why would the sheriff's wife be so angry? It wasn't as if he had taken advantage—or had he?

Lewis rolled onto his back and stared at the ceiling. As his fiancée, Catherine would have expected the kiss, pretending to be his fiancée, Clara would have known the kiss wasn't for her.

She'd only kissed him because she had to.

Suddenly, Emily's rant made sense.

Bone-headed was the least of the words he thought of to describe himself. He had taken advantage of sweet innocent Clara. Her deception aside, he'd forced her into a kiss. But the way she had responded, could it be that she wanted to be with him?

Lewis's hopes soared. Everything was working out better than he had ever planned. He would get the perfect preacher's wife after all.

⟫◆⟪

Clara found Mrs. Reese in the kitchen along with Nellie and Becky. "Good morning, Catherine."

At Mrs. Reese's greeting, Clara stiffened. She bit her lip for a moment, gathering courage. "Actually, my name is Clara. Catherine is the one who didn't come."

Becky dropped the pie tin she was drying. The clatter echoed through the kitchen.

"She asked me to pretend to be her for Lewis's sake." Clara hoped they wouldn't ask any questions.

"Well, that was unexpected," said Mrs. Reese. "And it explains much as well. I was going to advise you to wait on your nuptials if you continued to be so awkward around the Reverend Staples, who, oddly enough, sent word he wasn't coming this morning after all. Shame since we'd already started preparations for a large breakfast. The cinnamon buns won't be ready for another hour."

"How could your own fiancé not know who you are … o ain't?" asked Nellie.

Mrs. Reese frowned at the girl. "Grammar, Nellie. Ain't, however, fits this situation perfectly."

Clara rubbed the pendant at her throat. "That is an excellent question. One I mean to sort out first thing."

"So there won't be a wedding?" asked Becky.

There were too many unanswered questions, and despite the kiss—or because of it—Clara found her mind and heart in a battle for someone who didn't exist anymore. Maybe the man she'd fallen in love with never had. "I don't know."

Nellie plopped down in a chair. "I was making one of my special cakes."

Becky joined her. "I even made a new dress."

"Girls, don't pout at Clara. She isn't the reason the wedding has been called off."

"What about breakfast?" asked Becky.

Clara looked to Mrs. Reese for an answer. "We will still need to eat."

Mrs. Reese smiled. "And we should celebrate the arrival of our new teacher."

"Will you really be teaching us?" asked Becky.

"Yes. My agreement is with Emily and Rose's Rescue. I've brought ever so many books. Emily said some of you may want to learn German."

"You speak German? We've met people who speak it on market days." Becky gathered a breath and prepared to say more.

Nellie cut her off. "What about the reverend?"

"I don't know yet. I need to speak with him. Though it wouldn't be proper for me to go alone to his residence."

Nellie moved to the stove to stir something that hinted of raspberries. "One of those society rules I'm supposed to learn. Don't see how it applies to me. I'm ugly."

It was a truth that shouldn't be said out loud. If her face wasn't covered with scar tissue, Nellie would have been striking with her cinnamon-colored hair and green eyes. Could there be an appropriate response? "My mother always said that—" No, that thought was hardly helpful. "That good manners are a way of showing respect to others."

Nellie looked up from her stirring at Mrs. Reese. "I think she can stay. She didn't lie to me and try to tell me I ain't ugly or it's on the inside that matters."

"As a twin, I try not to judge too much on looks."

"Why not?" asked Becky.

"Because I am not the same as my sister. But side by side you'd be hard pressed to tell us apart. Most people don't care beyond looks." Bernard hadn't. Did Lewis? Were she and her sister as interchangeable as Catherine claimed?

"Do people really mix you up?" asked Becky.

Lewis had. If Catherine was to be believed. "My father had the worst time when we were little."

"Becky, while we finish the brunch, why don't you take a moment and show Miss Clara around town? She'll need to know where the Rescue is and where Miss Emily lives." Mrs. Reese suggested a way out of the kitchen but not all of the awkward conversation.

"Can I show her the church?"

"If she wants."

"Thank you, Becky. I would love to see where Emily lives. As well as the town. One minute, and I'll get a parasol."

"Becky, you should get yours too." Mrs. Reese pointed to the stand in the corner. Becky blew out a puff of air but obeyed.

Hiramsville was much as Clara had pictured it from the descriptions Emily and Lewis had sent. The largest building was by far the new three-story limestone courthouse sitting in the center of the town square. Courthouses were expected to be stately, and it didn't disappoint. Standing in the center of its own block surrounded by a lush new lawn, the building defined the town square. In time, the newly planted trees would shade the benches dotting the walkways leading from all directions to its doors. Separated by the street, shops and businesses ringed the square on all four sides, all facing the courthouse as if to honor the building.

"You should have seen it the day it was finished. There was a band and everything. My favorite part is the clock tower. I never have to wonder what time it is." Becky pointed to the large clock face. One could see for miles from the top of the clock tower which stood another three stories high above the attic level. Becky stood still admiring the structure.

"It is an impressive building." Clara hoped it was the complement Becky waited for. It must have been as Becky continued to the next corner where a much smaller stone building stood.

"Here is the jail where Miss Emily lives. The sheriff is almost done with their new house. I've never been upstairs to the jail, but there is supposed to be a gallows. Never been used though. State says all hangings have to happen — I forgot where— so they never used it. So, I suppose the place isn't haunted."

Emily swept the front stoop of the jailhouse. "Becky, what a story to tell my friend."

"I was going to show Miss Clara the mercantile and the theater next, I'm saving Rose's for last."

Emily raised her brow. "I'd say Miss Clara is starting her day off right then."

The two meanings to her friend's sentence were not lost on Clara. "Mornings are the best time for fresh starts. I apologize for any confusion about my identity yesterday."

"No bother for me. Have you seen the reverend yet?" asked Emily.

"Not yet," said Becky. "He is going to be in for—"

"Becky." Emily looked every inch the stern schoolmarm. "This is one of those times when you need to bite your tongue. Miss Clara has let you in on a great secret that is hers to share, not yours."

"But it is so exciting."

Clara touched Becky's arm. Everyone seemed to be so hard on the girl. "It is exciting that I am going to be a new teacher here. I don't mind you telling anyone that. However, Emily is correct. I would appreciate it if you let my friendship with the reverend be our secret for a while."

"But I thought Miss Emily already knew. She was with you so long last night."

"What if she didn't know?" asked Clara.

Becky's eyes widened. "Oh, I see."

Emily put an arm around Becky's waist. "You are doing a wonderful job of becoming a young lady."

"It is so hard. Is it true that girls in the East take classes on how to act properly?" Becky straightened as if someone had once coached her on posture.

"Some do." The most-hated way to spend an hour every day after school. "My mother and grandmother spent all of my life teaching my sister and me how to serve a proper luncheon, walk gracefully, and speak properly."

"Are you going to teach us all those things?" asked Becky.

"If by us you mean the students at Rose's, yes. Well, at least the things that matter. Walking about with books balanced on our heads was hardly helpful." A corset did as much for posture as a book.

Becky looked down at her feet. "Why do we need to know how to walk?"

Emily laid a hand on Becky's shoulder. "Why don't you come in, and I'll explain it."

Becky turned around. "Oh, good morning, Reverend. Mi—"

Emily pulled Becky into the jail as Lewis crossed the street.

"Good morning." He stepped uncomfortably close.

Clara had thought she was prepared for this moment. Now that it was here, the desire to run away overcame her. It took a moment for her to find her voice. "I'm glad you ran into us. We need to talk."

"Yes, we do. Would you care for a walk by the river?"

"I have a half hour before I need to return."

"The late breakfast, I assume?"

Afraid she might say something about him no longer coming, Clara nodded. Lewis offered his arm. Clara shook her head. "Considering I am not your fiancée, I don't think it is appropriate."

Lewis didn't register any shock at her announcement, leaving her with one option. "You knew?"

⟐◆⟐

Lewis led her around the corner into the side street before answering.

"I wasn't positive until I kissed you." The admission came easier than Lewis thought it would.

Clara closed her eyes and took a deep breath, a technique she'd used for years when she was upset. When she was six, she'd pinch her eyes closed tightly the same way she did when they played one of the many hiding games. When her lids rose, they revealed eyes the same color as the sea during a storm. Lewis took a small step backwards.

"Why didn't you ask?" Her voice shook.

"Would you have told me the truth?"

"I — I don't know. I think I would have. After all these years, I wanted to believe you couldn't mix us up. That you knew me. Why a kiss?"

Lewis stepped deeper into the side street, hoping no one would see them arguing. "I should apologize for the kiss. Emily, I mean Mrs. Morgan, says I shouldn't have taken liberties."

"Are you apologizing because you think you ought to? Or because you regret it?"

"How can I regret the kiss? It was everything divine. Just as I always knew it would be with you."

Clara's hand balled in a fist. "What are you talking about? How could you kiss me when you are engaged to her? And to admit you thought of kissing me?"

"Our engagement was an accident?" The statement sounded less sure than he planned. The conversation wasn't going as he hoped. She was supposed to be delighted that he knew he'd kissed her, not angered. Then she would agree to marry him.

"How can being engaged to someone for a year be an accident?" Anger dried the tears from her eyes before he could.

"I thought I was proposing to you."

"Then why didn't you say something?" She poked his chest with each word.

"I'd already kissed Catherine, or she'd kissed me."

"And that prevented you from correcting things?" Anger radiated off her in waves. In all the years he'd known Clara, he'd never seen her fight for her place. The powerful storm behind her eyes gave her a power he wished to hold.

"I thought I was doing the right thing. I thought it was God's will that I marry her instead."

"God's will? Of all the stupid …" She paused to collect herself again. "I don't mean God; he isn't stupid. Catherine never wanted to marry you. I did. I always did. Do you know how painful it was to have her mock your letters? She longed for a way out. She found it. Don't you understand? I only stepped out with Bernard because I was trying to forget you. He only wanted to talk with Catherine, who, once the novelty of being engaged wore off, thought only of the parties she was missing. I spent a year trying to understand why I wasn't enough for you. You were the one person who—who" She shook her head and took a deep breath. "—It doesn't matter. I hope you are as miserable as you deserve to be." She spun on her heel and rushed away.

Lewis caught up with Clara in three strides and grabbed her elbow. "I didn't mean to hurt you, her, us. Please let me explain?"

"What is there you can say that will change things? You used to stand up for yourself and me. Our coming-out dance—" Clara choked back a sob and turned to face one of the large shade trees behind the jail.

She'd been beautiful that night. Both sisters had been. Even his own sister had looked stunning at the ball meant to launch them into Boston society. He'd been at Harvard for a year and on the cusp of switching to the smaller seminary. As was his duty, he danced with both of the twins early in the evening. As the night wore on, Catherine claimed the lion's share of the dances. Most of her partners vied to be the first on the floor, putting her at the head of reel after reel. It hadn't taken him long to realize that her sister even waylaid men who were trying to dance with Clara leaving her to dance with the men who remained. For the last dance, he positioned himself to lead Clara to the floor first, an honor the quieter sister deserved. During that waltz, the five years' difference between them melted away. No longer had she been the pesky little girl next door, she was the intriguing young woman he wanted to know better. Only Clifford had kept him from pushing the relationship past the friendship they'd always shared.

Lewis relaxed his grip on her arm. "I'm sorry. I never meant to hurt you."

"But you did." The fierceness in her face softened, and she stepped back. "You should have —"

"I should have done so many things. I didn't. I thought it was you who eloped."

"Catherine's letter?"

He nodded. "I know you won't believe me. I was going to break the engagement. Then I realized that you were pretending to be her, and all the problems were solved. You are here, and I don't have to explain to anyone."

"You assume I'll just marry you?"

"Why else would you have pretended to be Catherine? And it works out so easily."

"For you." She shook her head. "You've changed, Lewis. I don't know you anymore."

"I'm the same person."

"The same person who used to help me out of trees and choose me for games when the others left me out? No, Lewis, you are not. You are not the man who convinced my father that it was Catherine's fault that the Chinese vase fell. You are not the same man who discussed theology with me in German. You are but a shadow of him. The Lewis I know would have fought for me last year when he realized Catherine duped him. The Lewis I knew as a girl would have fought for me if he really wanted me, not kept a year-long engagement with Catherine."

"So you won't marry me?" Logically, a marriage solved everything. They could get married, and he could keep his job. She would have a husband. Didn't every woman want one?

"Why would I marry you?"

Not what he expected. "Isn't that why you are here? Why you posed as Catherine yesterday?"

"I don't want you to lose your position, but I am not willing to live a lie either. I realized that last night. I thought I had to do what Catherine asked. It was hard enough to be her yesterday. I'm not her."

"I know you're not Catherine. You're the one I want to marry. Marry me, Clara." He could show her the letters he'd written the other morning, maybe then she'd understand.

"No." Her firm answer echoed through him.

"Why not?"

"Because I am tired of being the other twin, the second choice." There were tears in her eyes.

"I don't understand."

She stepped away from him. "Perhaps if I had done this the other way I imagined, it would have been easier."

"What way was that?"

She took another step back just out of reach. "I should slap you for taking that kiss."

She didn't raise her hand. Instead she turned and ran up the street leaving him to stare after her. She'd been correct in that old letter. Meekness wasn't weakness.

It had never occurred to him that Clara would tell him no. What was he to do? He needed a wife. Even though he'd dated the letters, she wasn't likely to believe them now. She needed something more, something he didn't understand how to give.

If not Clara, who?

No one.

He had no interest in the few single women in the congregation. None of them had Clara's intelligence or her smile.

He walked down the street until he came to the mighty Brazos River.

Lewis stared as the water rolled by. Aware that although the river didn't seem to change, the water that was here a moment ago was now down at the bend, moving on, leaving him behind. He couldn't quite wrap his mind around what the metaphor meant for him.

Clara had also changed. She stood up to him and had walked away. Why would she make everything more difficult? He'd apologized. They were meant to be together.

A twig floated by and was hopelessly caught in an eddy. There was his metaphor. He was a stick tossed about by the river. Not a very pleasant thought.

He almost wished she had slapped him as she had seemed about to do.

The pain from a slap would have ended.

The feeling of uncertainty would not.

lara pinned her hair up in the simple fashion she preferred, bracing herself for the day ahead.

Hiramsville needed more than one church. If only so Clara would not have to sit among the congregation today. Skipping Sunday services was not an option. No matter what Lewis said, her introduction to the town would be awkward for one or both of them. A few people had seen them at the station. Hopefully, no one had witnessed the kiss that had kept her awake for the past two nights as she tried to sort it out.

She'd never been introduced to a congregation or anyone really without her sister at her side. No one would be looking at her to determine who was the tallest or had the straightest nose. She would just be Clara. Not the less musical one. Not the one with scars on her knees. Not the quiet or shy one. She would be the sister of the one who'd jilted the minister, but that was not her fault. He wouldn't dare mention his disaster of a proposal, if that was what it was. Proposals should make a woman feel cherished, not the solution to a man's problems—problems he caused.

Clara had spent much of yesterday unpacking her trunks. Emily had her husband and brother-in-law deliver the one Lewis had stored at the manse. It had saved her from facing Lewis again. She'd only managed to express part of her thoughts and emotions to him yesterday. The more she thought about how she felt, the more she realized her thoughts and feelings were tangled like the bits of leftover floss in her sewing bag—an impossible set of knots she couldn't loosen without pulling on others.

Lewis didn't love her. If he did, he would have known who she was. Marriages should have at least some notion of feeling between the husband and wife.

Someone tapped on her bedroom door.

"Come in."

Becky stuck her head in. "Mrs. Reese says it is time to go."

Clara checked her hat in the mirror and picked up her Bible from the dressing table.

Mrs. Reese waited in the entry hall. "Several weeks ago, I invited Reverend Staples to dine with us today. Should I find another family to feed him?" Parishioners must take turns feeding their bachelor pastor.

"No, it will be rather convenient as I have some things his mother sent for him. We are old friends and neighbors." At least that was the face she must put on for everyone.

Mrs. Reese stepped onto the porch and lifted her parasol. "We normally walk to church unless we have too much to carry. I find it cruel to make the horses stand for two hours so that I don't have to walk a few blocks."

"Very sensible." Clara had never thought about it, but then again it had been Father's choice how they'd arrived at church.

"Becky, you may be seen home by someone as long as you inform me."

Clara looked from the girl to the matron. There was much more to the story than employee and employer. "Where is Nellie?"

"She is over at Rose's. She doesn't feel comfortable worshiping with us so she holds her own service for the others who feel the same. You should listen to her sing. Her mother sang like an angel too. In a different place and time, they would have had very different lives."

"What do you mean?"

"Nellie was born in a brothel. Her mother was the most sought-after of all the girls. I suppose she got there the way most women do. She wanted something different for her daughter. But men started looking at Nellie when she was far too young. Nellie's mother was addicted to opium by then and did the only thing she could think of to save her daughter from the life she loathed. Up until then, Nellie had been going to school and occasionally even to Sunday school. But she had no friends because overzealous mothers kept their children away. After Nellie was scarred, she wasn't welcome anywhere in public. Nellie's mother died not long after. I offered to take the child in, but she was more comfortable in the kitchen at Belle's. As far as I know, her mother's idea did save Nellie from a life of prostitution, but it left her with another kind of pain. Pain that some of our good citizens inflict. I'm glad to see that you didn't judge her for her scars."

"What a difficult choice for her mother." Clara couldn't imagine disfiguring her own child.

"Life is full of choices. It is the consequences that are difficult," said Mrs. Reese.

They turned down the street to the church. The white wooden building was similar to those in the East.

"Reverend Green is here today." Becky pointed to a buggy.

"Who is Reverend Green?"

"He is our old preacher." Becky smiled broadly. "He is so nice."

Mrs. Reese leaned closer to Clara. "Mostly retired now. His rheumatism flares up and makes it difficult to get out much. Last winter, he was ill with pneumonia, which still plagues him. He moved a few miles downriver where there is a small community of a couple dozen homes, but no church. He was going to be the one to conduct Reverend Staples's wedding ceremony."

Music greeted the congregants as they entered. Emily smiled at Clara from behind the harmonium she played. Though not as grand as the church organs she was used to, the smaller instrument provided a reverent backdrop as they entered. Clara followed Mrs. Reese into a pew, aware that almost everyone's eyes were on her.

At precisely ten o'clock, according to the courthouse bell tower, Emily concluded her hymn, and Lewis stood to welcome the congregation. Clara's spine stiffened. What would he say about her?

"Welcome to another Sabbath. I would like to extend a special welcome to Miss Clara Taylor who is here to teach at Rose's Rescue. I know a number of you assumed Clara was my bride, however Miss Catherine Taylor has chosen a different path for her life and didn't come to Hiramsville. This also means that this Wednesday's wedding has been canceled."

Whispers and groans echoed through the small chapel.

"Many of you were looking forward most specifically to the dinner on Wednesday and the chance to socialize. The church committee has suggested that we still have the dinner as planned since some of our best cooks have already started preparations. Now, if you will turn to page thirty-four in your hymnal..."

"I bet three," said Becky under her breath.

Clara looked from the hymnal to Becky and back. The hymn only had two verses. "Three what?"

"Proposals before the day is out."

"What do you mean?"

"I bet three men will propose to you today. I'd say four, but Mr. Collins isn't here."

"Why would someone propose to me when they haven't met me?"

"The single men outnumber the single women."

"Hush." Mrs. Reese's scolding was in tune with the final note of the hymn.

Clara had never heard Lewis preach before or even speak in public. He had a good preaching voice. Not too loud. She detested the vibrato some preachers used to make their voices resonate. He explained the verses of his text, clearly, inviting each to think of how they would react to Christ's words. His examples contained enough humor to keep his congregation engaged. Of course, since she was studying him, the content of his sermon was mostly lost on her. As he concluded, she hoped no one would quiz her about the subject.

They sang the final hymn, and the older Reverend pronounced a benediction. A few of the parishioners, mostly females, pushed to the front of the chapel.

Mrs. Reese leaned over. "I bet two proposals for the preacher."

"That doesn't make sense. If there are so few women that you expect I'll get three proposals, how would he get two?"

Mrs. Reese nodded to the front. "Their mothers keep their daughters away from the locals. But a preacher? They've been waiting for a year to get their claws into him. He'd be a good son-in-law. Let's get you out of here before you can't move."

Clara's way was blocked by several people all trying to greet her. By the time she exited the building, she'd met more people than the building could hold. Her mind knew it was an exaggeration, even if it felt real.

More people waited outside.

Mrs. Reese stayed by her side although Becky disappeared with a young man with more pimples than whiskers. Mrs. Reese navigated through the crowd faster than Clara thought possible.

Halfway home, she realized not one person had asked about her sister. In fact, she'd gone all morning without a single reference to her twin. She had just been Clara. How odd. In that moment, she also keenly felt her sister's absence as she did each night when she went to bed alone in her room.

It was oddly exhilarating, being alone without Catherine a few feet away. They had never been apart this long. If only they could talk. Did Catherine turn her head every few minutes to say something to the sister who wasn't there? Or was she too busy with her new husband? Perhaps Bernard filled the void in Catherine's life that Clara had discovered in hers.

Mrs. Reese made a comment about the sermon. Clara nodded. Thankfully, she had friends in her new home.

⟫◈⟪

The news that he was no longer engaged had a peculiar effect on Lewis's congregation. One that left Reverend Green chuckling in the manse's parlor long after services were over.

"It is not that funny." Lewis carried a lopsided cake to the kitchen.

"You should have no shortage of food now."

"How much of it will be edible?"

"Most. Their mothers will be sure of it."

"Mothers? Thelma Lou is barely fifteen, if she is a day. I can't believe her mother sent her here—alone no less."

"And this is why our leaders prefer to send married men to shepherd these small parishes."

"What am I going to do? I like Hiramsville and don't want to have to leave." Returning to Austin or one of the other larger churches and being a junior pastor again—or worse, a clerk—was not where he wanted to be. He'd already spent three months in Austin as a junior, a position that seemed barely better than being a butler with a dog collar. The six months he'd been under Reverend Green's tutelage had been much easier. The last three months leading the congregation had brought him more joy than he'd thought a responsibility could.

"I don't want you to leave either. A few of the ministers they sent out for trial runs were not a good fit. I want Rose's Rescue to succeed, and there are still many minds to change." Reverend Green coughed into his handkerchief.

"I don't understand why it is so controversial. Giving women a chance to escape the brothels should be on every benevolent society's list of causes."

"It is, in theory, as long as it is in someone else's city, near someone else's husband."

"We have won over so many people to the idea." More than half of the congregation had donated to help with the Rescue. "We need more time."

"It won't help if you are sent back. I'd have to get another preacher all fired up. However, I have a solution." Reverend Green coughed again.

Lewis waited for the coughing fit to end.

"If I moved back into the manse with you, that would solve some of the leadership's concerns. You would become a junior again in name only since I am not well enough to take the majority of the load."

"I thought you liked it down in your little cabin at de Cordova bend."

Reverend Green had moved to a small cabin ten miles down the Brazos where a community had sprung up just after the new year in hopes of setting up a church for the farmers moving to the area.

"The seven families there don't want a church. They barely tolerate me."

"I thought there were a dozen families down there."

"There were. But one got burned out, and the others left willingly. They need a lawman down there, not a preacher. I believe the ones that are left are the ones driving the others out."

"Why?"

"It's good land. That bend in the Brazos has some of the richest soil I've seen."

Lewis pondered the answer for a moment. Land wars weren't uncommon. "Do you want to come back up here?"

"I'd like to be around more people. I'd rather die doing some good in this world than sitting on my front porch watching pecan trees grow."

"If you move up here it will give me time to convince Clara that marrying me is a good option."

Reverend Green coughed again. "You're thinking about this all wrong. I've counseled enough couples in my time to know you can't convince a woman to marry you."

"But I need a wife."

"What does she need?"

"A husband."

"Why?"

"All women need husbands."

"So say the men of this world. What does she really need? She has a job. So she doesn't need a husband to provide food and shelter."

Lewis's brow furrowed as he turned the question over in his mind. He needed a wife to keep his job and to fulfill

God's commandment to Adam, as the church put it. Having a family was a noble thing. Didn't Clara need these same things?

"Ah, good. I see you are thinking. I don't expect the answer will come easy."

"I have no idea what she wants."

"Needs, not wants. The two words are different. Sometimes they work together. Other times they are at cross-purposes. How many men want to be rich?"

"Most."

"How many rich men are happy and content with their life?"

"Judging from my father's circle, not many."

"No one needs to be wealthy. However, everyone needs enough money to know that tomorrow there will be food on the table and a roof that doesn't leak overhead. A wise man will not want much beyond his needs."

"I see what you mean."

The reverend coughed again. "If you don't mind, I think I will have a bit of a nap. What room shall I use?"

"Your old room." Lewis intended to wait until he was married to take over the larger bedroom Reverend Green had once shared with his wife. After thoroughly cleaning it last week, he'd planned on moving most of his things in tomorrow.

"Good. It will now be mine. If there are visitors, we can sort out sleeping arrangements. I am sure someone will come up from Austin when the news of your canceled engagement reaches them."

Not a visit to look forward to. Lewis would be in danger of a demotion until he was wed. They could even send him back to the seminary.

"Should we ride out and get your things today?"

"Don't you have dinner plans?"

"Mrs. Reese invited me. Since the circumstances have changed, I doubt they will miss me."

"Miss Clara boards with Mrs. Reese?"

"Yes."

"It's rude to stand a parishioner up. Even if you are avoiding people at the table. We will get my things tomorrow." Reverend Green mounted the staircase. The third step squeaked and he tested his weight on it, creating more squeaks. "I see you couldn't fix it either."

Lewis hadn't tried, as he often took the stairs two at a time to avoid the loud stair. The cuckoo clock he'd acquired during his trip to Europe chirped at him, reminding him it was time to leave. He checked his hat in the mirror by the door.

Cutting through alleyways, Lewis hurried to Mrs. Reese's home. Becky answered the door. "Afternoon, preacher. Supper is ready. We were just about to sit down."

Lewis hung his hat on the rack near the door.

Becky's welcoming grin grew. "Nellie bet me a slice of lemon pie you wouldn't come."

He was about to remind the girl she shouldn't bet when Clara descended the stairs.

Lewis's mouth dried up like the sands at the base of Comanche Peak. He didn't dare speak. When had she become so beautiful?

Clara's knuckles whitened as she tightened her grip on the banister, willing her surprise not to show. Although she hadn't joined in the wagering with the girls, Clara had agreed with Nellie that Lewis would not come to dinner. As her foot landed on the last step, she spoke since no one else did. "Good afternoon, Reverend."

Lewis only nodded at her. If he was not to speak, it would be better if he had not come at all. The rules of society they grew up in dictated he offer his arm to escort her into the dining room. Instead, he stood dumbly next to Becky who tried to urge him forward.

"I believe that our dinner awaits." Without waiting for Lewis to move, Clara entered the dining room. The seats were not assigned. Unsure where she should sit, Clara stood behind the seat next to Mrs. Reese who sat at the head of the table.

Becky and Lewis took their time entering the dining room. Whispers of conversation reached her ears. Clara could not make out the words. She assumed Lewis was attempting to make his excuses and leave. Those already gathered around the table waited almost a full minute for his entrance.

"Welcome, Reverend." Mrs. Reese gestured at the chair at the foot of the table.

Becky looked at the chair in front of Clara rather than at Mrs. Reese. Mrs. Reese inclined her head to the chair closest to Lewis indicating that Becky should sit there. Nellie took the single seat opposite of them and closer to the kitchen.

Once seated, Mrs. Reese asked Clara to lead grace. Clara repeated a prayer they had used often at Bradford College before meals.

It took a moment for Clara to realize that, like yesterday no one would be serving the meal. Instead, each person took a bit of whatever was in front of them and passed it around. Serving themselves thus made Clara happier at her seat choice. For if she had been sitting next to Lewis, the chances that their hands would bump or his fingers brush against hers would be too great.

Conversation was slow to start. Nellie and Becky exchanged many glances, communicating without words. Clara assumed the looks that passed between the two young women were all about who'd won the wager and the size of the slice of lemon pie Becky wanted.

Mrs. Reese broke the silence. "I was surprised to see Reverend Green here today."

"He will be staying with me for the foreseeable future. It seems the settlement he moved to is not what he'd hoped." Lewis's speech carried a bit of something that softened his normal Boston clipped tones.

"I've heard rumors that things were not going well down near de Cordova bend." Mrs. Reese took a roll and passed the basket on to Clara.

Lewis set the meat platter down on the trivet. "Several families have abandoned the area. He believes it is best that he leaves as well."

"Where will he go?" asked Becky.

"He will come here and live with me."

"Will he be over our congregation then?" asked Mrs. Reese.

Lewis shrugged and sipped from his glass. "That remains to be seen. Neither of us are sure what they will do with me, now that I am a bachelor again."

Becky's fork threatened to drop its piece of meat as she held it in the air. "How soon will you know?"

"Reverend Green and I will write tomorrow explaining the situation. I expect to know in two or three weeks. He believes that his presence will allow me to maintain my post for at least a while." He looked in Clara's direction.

At least she hadn't cost him his job, yet. Clara spent as long buttering her roll as possible. She had very little to add to this part of the conversation. Guilt niggled at Clara's heart. She could prevent this. Yet it was not her fault. He had proposed to Catherine, not her. The odd proposal yesterday didn't count. Their past of him bandaging childhood scrapes and long chats did not mean she owed him the rest of her life. Lewis was little more than a stranger anymore to her. Maybe she'd built him up too much in her daydreams in her youth, but by the time she'd known she had feelings for him, they were too old to see each other often. Or at least he had been, since he was away at school.

"I hope they let you stay," said Nellie. "I was just getting used to you. I like that you come and give a sermon at Rose's."

"And I like that you serve dessert." Lewis's smile held a genuine warmth.

"Do you give the same sermon that you give in the morning?" asked Clara.

"Sometimes. It depends on my subject. I feel my message should be one of encouragement to the women at Rose's, and there are times when the congregation needs to hear harder truths." Lewis paused for a moment. "As a teacher, you are welcome to come."

"You should come with us, Clara. Nellie and I always go," said Becky.

"Becky only comes for the food," said Nellie.

Mrs. Reese touched Nellie's hand. "You know that isn't true."

"We'll see. Tonight, Miss Lavender is making rice pudding for dessert." Nellie leveled a glare at Becky.

Becky grimaced. "With raisins?"

"Yes."

Becky shuddered. "Then I will only go for the sermon. Reverend, you may have my pudding if you wish."

"You just don't like rice pudding." Nellie made a face like she was scrunching up her nose; however, the scars prevented it from being as serious as it should've been.

Becky stuck out her tongue.

"Girls! If you are going to act like children, you will be sent to your room." Mrs. Reese dabbed at her mouth with her napkin. From her perspective, Clara saw she was hiding a smile.

Lewis also dabbed his mouth, the same left right left way his mother did. The action reminded Clara of some things she forgot. "Lewis—I mean, Reverend —"

"We are old friends. You may call me Lewis."

"Your mother sent along some things I was to pass on to you. I will get them after dinner."

Nellie picked up the platter. "You may as well go get it now. It'll take me a few minutes to get dessert ready."

"Becky, help Nellie." Mrs. Reese shooed the girls out of the room. "I miss Thelma. She'll be back this week. She's such a calming influence on the girls."

"She went to Galveston?" asked Lewis.

"Yes." Mrs. Reese inclined her head to Clara. "I am sure

you will love Thelma as much as I do. If not for her wit, then for her cooking—although Nellie is so much improved over the past year."

"I look forward to meeting her. If you will excuse me, I'll fetch the reverend's things." Clara set her napkin on the table and hurried from the room and upstairs to her own. Lewis's old satchel sat where she'd left it on her half-empty trunk. Much of what remained inside the trunk belonged to Catherine like linens for setting up house and such.

Clara returned quickly, clutching the satchel. To her surprise, Lewis waited at the bottom of the stairs. "I am taking my leave."

"Before dessert? I hope you're not leaving on my account."

"No, our dinner discussion merely reminded me that I had meant to make a slight alteration to my sermon before delivering it this evening at the Rescue."

Clara handed Lewis the satchel. "Your mother sent this."

"I asked for it, but I assumed it would've been in Catherine's things."

"Catherine insisted I take it." She had almost a whole trunk of things Catherine insisted she take. What to do with them now, Clara was still unsure. She could hardly use the wedding gifts that had been given to Catherine; they must be returned.

"I am glad it is not lost. But I am beginning to wonder if I ever knew your sister at all."

"I have wondered the same thing."

"Do you suppose she will write soon?"

"I can only hope so. I spent much of the afternoon trying to write Mother and Father." Not wanting to cast her sister in a poor light, the letter was taking far longer to write than it should.

"Do you suppose that she told your parents that you were the one who ran off?"

"You know her better than you think. That is exactly what she said she did." *I do not understand why she had to ruin my reputation too.* So strong was the thought that Clara was surprised she managed to keep from uttering it.

"Do you think it would help if I were to write and say that only you arrived here?"

Clara bit her lip. "As much as I don't wish to anger my parents, it may help to have a second witness that I am here."

"I was thinking I needed to write to your father anyway, to formally end the engagement." His words hung awkwardly in the air between them.

What else could she say? She couldn't marry him just to help him save face or for his job. All of Brookline would be buzzing with the gossip long before their letters arrived. Surely some of the maids would have overheard Father when he read Catherine's letter telling of Clara's elopement. "Thank you. My poor mother will not know what to think."

"With your permission, I will write my mother with as much of the story as I know. She may be of some comfort to your family."

"I am truly sorry. I wish —" Clara had no idea what she wished. In order for things to be different, she would have to wish away an entire year.

"I shall take my leave," he repeated his earlier words. Lewis turned to the door and let himself out. A moment later, he knocked and reopened the door. "I forgot my hat."

Clara continued to stand on the bottom stair for some time after the screen door closed. A dozen if onlys clouded her mind—the biggest being if only Lewis's words matched the kiss, she would have married him this Wednesday.

⎯⎯⎯◈⎯⎯⎯

Most of the people who attended the evening sermon were tied to Rose's Rescue in one way or another. It had taken weeks for them to accept Lewis among their ranks and welcome his sermons. Most of the women, and in two cases their children, who took refuge in the brothel-turned-trade-school were unwilling to attend regular services for various reasons. The foremost being the fear of running into a former client—or worse, a client's wife. As usual, Emily Morgan greeted all who entered. By her side, stood her husband TJ, without his sheriff's star, for the service.

In the back corner, a new addition to Rose's Rescue studied the crowd.

Lewis knew it would take her time to realize that her former life couldn't reach her here. He'd seen several of the women and girls show the same anxiety their first days, and sometimes weeks, at Rose's.

Clara entered with Nellie and Becky. The two girls wasted no time in introducing the new teacher around.

As the clock in the town square chimed a seventh time, Nellie crossed the room to the piano and played the first notes of "Amazing Grace." Hardly a week went by when the hymn wasn't played. Most of the women joined in singing under Emily's direction.

Unlike the morning service, there was no need for announcements. However, Lewis felt the need to make one before he delivered his sermon. "I hope you all had the chance to meet Miss Clara. You may have heard the rumors by now—her sister, Catherine, didn't come to Texas. Because many of Hiramsville's best cooks and bakers have already started preparations for a dinner on Wednesday, we will be having a social, although there will be no wedding. You are all invited."

Lewis launched into his sermon which featured Rahab as a lesson on how God could use anyone to help him accomplish his purposes. At the conclusion of the sermon, Nellie played another hymn. It was not until the rice pudding was served that Lewis realized that his announcement had garnered more attention than the sermon.

Miss Petunia approached him with her six-month-old son balanced on her hip. Petunia, like many of the women, changed her name when coming to the Rescue. To honor Rose, most of them chose flower names if they hadn't been known by one in their profession. "Preacher, is it true you be lookin' for a wife now?"

How had he not foreseen this reaction to his announcement? While some of the women at the Rescue desired to learn a trade and never be beholden to a man again, others hoped for nothing more than to catch a husband to care for them. Petunia fell in the latter category.

"Not just yet. There are still many questions about my bride's failure to come that must be answered."

"Oh." Petunia's bright smile wavered. The baby reached out a slobbery hand to Lewis, which he avoided taking since such a gesture could be seen as encouragement.

Becky came over with a tray of puddings, saving Lewis from an awkward conversation. "Here you are. Miss Petunia, would you like one for Scotty? Miss Lavender made one without raisins for him."

"How kind of her. Will you set them on the table for me?"

Lewis stepped back to allow Becky room and was swept into a new conversation.

"Preacher, I was telling the new girl that you don't preach fire and brimstone to us and she asked me why. And, I don't rightly know." Miss Peony had been one of Belle's girls and the one to suggest using flower names.

"Miss Peony, that is because Christ told the women in adultery to go and sin no more. You have all chosen to come here, so I don't believe that I should spend our time together telling you something you already know."

"The story you told tonight. God really saved a harlot?" asked Miss Peony.

"You mean Rahab? That is what the Bible says," said Lewis.

"What about the men who forced her into it?" asked Miss Lavender.

"The Bible says everyone was destroyed except her family she had with her. I'll have to assume the men were destroyed too." He'd never thought about the story from their perspective.

"That's a heap to think on." Miss Daffodil pointed at Clara. "Have you met the new teacher? She seems to be a fine lady."

"I believe she is. Miss Taylor was my neighbor in Boston." He had no intention of telling them her sister was to marry him if the women didn't already know.

"Miss Emily says she will teach us German so we can take our things to the German market to sell. How did she learn German?" asked Miss Daffodil.

"I believe she learned it at school. She went to the same school Miss Emily did."

Miss Peony tilted her head. "But Miss Emily knows French."

"Some women's colleges teach many languages," said Lewis.

"How many languages are there?" asked Miss Peony.

Lewis had never thought about it before. "I have no idea."

The new girl who looked to be younger than Becky spoke at last. "I thought preachers knew everything."

"I hope that isn't a requirement. There are many things I don't know."

"Like what?" she asked.

"Your name."

"I don't got one yet. I liked your story about Rahab. But her name is just silly."

"You didn't want a flower name?" asked Lewis.

"I don't like flowers."

More than likely, whomever she worked for had changed her name to Daisy, Violet, or some other common flower. "How about Rae? Short for Rahab."

"I guess that could work." She turned to Miss Lavender. "My name is Rae."

Lewis stepped away as the women and girls welcomed Rae by her new name. He found TJ near the door.

"Good job, preacher. Emily was beginning to despair that she would never choose a name. Took her a whole day to talk. If I have my badge on, she runs from the room."

"I'm surprised she spoke with me."

"I am too. There is more to that girl than meets the eye. I keep thinking…" TJ let his sentence die and shook his head.

"How old is she?"

"Claims to be nineteen, but she looks younger. Caught her lurking around the train station several times this week. Says she's waiting for something."

The crowd around Rae broke up.

Becky leaned against the wall and crossed her arms. "Nellie is going to stay here tonight."

Lewis nodded. He'd learned not to get mixed up in the quarrels between Becky and Nellie as he rarely understood what they were about.

Clara approached. "Nellie said you were ready to leave."

With a grunt, Becky pushed off the wall and exited. Clara hurried after her.

"You could escort them home." TJ pointed out the obvious.

"It's still light. No one will bother them."

"It would give you a chance to look at her instead of pretending she isn't in the room."

Lewis didn't ask who. "That obvious?"

"Preacher, you made eye contact with everyone in the room except for Miss Clara during your sermon. You didn't say a word to her, even though you had a chance more than once. I may not know much about women, but I do know that isn't a good way to show you are interested."

"She isn't interested in me."

"Oh?" TJ raised a brow. "The way her eyes followed you around the room, I wouldn't think that."

"Really?" Clara had watched him. How had he not noticed? Of course he didn't dare pay her too much attention, not here.

TJ nodded once before Emily joined them.

"I'd ask what you two are discussing, but I don't want my evening ruined. TJ, will you take me home?"

Lewis left with them. Being the only man in a room of single women was never a good idea.

everal men tipped their hats to her as Clara walked to her first day of work, but no one attempted to speak with her. Much to Clara's relief, Becky's prediction of proposals hadn't come true. According to Mrs. Reese, she'd missed two callers while at last evening's service. Never had attending an evening service been met with a more immediate reward. Sooner or later, she would need to let people know she wasn't interested in a quick marriage. Perhaps the men would figure it out themselves.

From a distance Rose's Rescue still looked like other saloons Clara had seen through the train's windows. Although Emily and others had repainted the building, it was not difficult to imagine men gambling in the main room or ordering drinks, although there was no bar along the side wall.

She found Emily in an office off of the main room. Emily looked up as she entered. "Good morning. Ready for your first day?"

"I don't have any lesson plans, and I'm not sure of what I am teaching beyond some German."

"In the mornings, we study reading, writing, and math; focusing on basic bookkeeping and geometry. Knowing the radius of a circle comes in very handy in dress making. You'll find the skill levels range from non-existent to as much schooling as you. Miss Lavender attended a college in Pennsylvania."

"How did she—"

Emily held up her hand. "They will share their stories with you when they are ready. I will only share pertinent details. Having narrowly escaped being among their ranks has allowed me to build some credibility and trust. I'm afraid you will have to earn their trust yourself."

"I understand."

"It is a very thin line that separates a woman's fate in this world."

"'But for the grace of God go I'?" Clara quoted the popular saying.

"Yes. Our job is to help provide that grace to give these women and girls a new place to go. We don't judge and we don't force. Best of all we don't give marks. Whenever possible, have a student who understands a concept teach that concept. For example, have your beginning readers teach the alphabet, and your advanced readers teach grammar. Not only do the women respond better to their peers, when they teach it helps them understand better."

"So where do you want me to start?"

"Observe this morning and then this afternoon you can start teaching basic German. I should warn you that a few of them do know some German phrases, all related to their former work. Try not to register shock if they use curse words in any language. Like Nellie, some grew up in brothels and were put to work before they were even ten. They will test you to see how accepting you are. Remember they all asked to be here and are daughters of the King and Lord of all." Emily stood and straightened her skirts. "We start our day with a devotional. I think it is Miss Petunia's turn to lead us."

Clara took a deep breath and hoped none of her nervousness showed. If someone mistook her apprehension to teach in her first post for reluctance to teach them, it could be disastrous. She followed Emily to the main room. Rather than the rows of desks or benches found in many schools, the Rescue used the round tables, that once seated gamblers and drunks, to hold the classes. Teachers didn't stand in front of the room but became equals sitting with students. Miss Lavender taught most of the day, leaving Clara to question the need for a new teacher. Nellie and Becky joined in the academic lessons. In the afternoon, Nellie taught restaurant style cooking, while Becky helped with the sewing on the three Singer sewing machines. The women not only outfitted themselves, but they also constructed clothing which they sold to stores in Dallas and Austin.

As the heat of the day warmed the building, Emily gathered all the women for their afternoon reading. Nellie and some helpers served iced lemonade and tea as they took turns reading from *Around the World in Eighty Days* by the French writer Jules Verne.

Emily handed Clara the book and asked her to read the next chapter. Halfway through the second page, one of the women giggled. A few moments later, another woman covered her mouth to suppress a laugh.

Clara slowed her reading, sending a quick glance to Emily, who signaled for her to continue. Clara finished her assigned pages and handed the book back.

"I never heard no one read that way," said Rae.

Clara read as she always had.

"You did all the voices," said Becky. "My mother did voices. How do you do that?"

"My twin sister and I always read that way. I guess it is a habit. Is that why you were laughing?"

"I tried not to—I didn't want you to think I was rude—but when that deep man's voice came out of you, I couldn't believe it." Nellie's smile was worth the momentary embarrassment.

"Will you read some more?" asked Miss Peony.

Emily stood. "Our reading time is over for the day. Miss Clara will be starting our German class soon, and she is teaching us to count to ten."

Clara's mind raced. She hadn't prepared to teach, although Emily had chosen an easy topic. Since the students were at several tables, Clara stood. "Before I teach you the numbers, I should teach you the word for 'no' which is 'nein' which sounds like our number nine and can lead to some confusion since they say nine as 'neun' which sounds similar to 'nein.'"

Becky raised her hand. "They all sound the same to me."

"They did to me at first, too. It helps me to remember the context. If we are discussing the number of potatoes we need to buy the answer is more likely to be a number rather than 'no.'" Clara continued the lesson and soon everyone was counting from eins to zehn.

When the practice devolved into chatting, Emily clapped her hands for attention. "Class is over for the day. Just a reminder to check the duties board. Assignments rotate tomorrow."

There was a general groan from the group.

The front door swung open with a bang. Two filthy men entered and took several steps inside before stopping in confusion. A boy peeked in the door and darted off.

"Whiskey?" The larger man's bellow held a note of question.

The skinny one's face stretched into a hungry smile. "Look at all these women. Belle's got a fresh batch."

"Gentlemen." Emily's greeting couldn't be further from the truth. "I believe you are in the wrong place."

"Nah, this is Belle's." The skinny man pointed at Nellie. "I remember her ugly mug."

"You are mistaken. Clarabelle LaBlanc is in prison." Emily took a step toward them while some of the other women slipped out of the room. "This is a private school. I suggest you leave."

The men looked around, their faces slack. The larger man stared at the near wall as if willing the removed bar to reappear there. He nodded to Emily. "Many pardons, ma'am."

A deputy arrived with the boy as the men stepped off the boardwalk. Clara couldn't hear the conversation which was punctuated with pointing, and the deputy directing the men down the cross street.

The boy followed the deputy through the door. "Any problem, Miss Emily?"

"Only a bit of confusion. They left peacefully." Emily handed the boy a coin. "Thanks, Donny."

"You know this will keep happening as long as you are using Belle's place," said the deputy.

"So, you have pointed out before. However, this is only the second time this month we have had unwelcome visitors." Emily spoke as if the annoyance was nothing more than a fly at a picnic.

The deputy cast a glare around the room and stomped out. The women resumed their activities as if nothing happened.

Unsure what her role was now, Clara worked her way through the room to Emily. "What more do you need me to do?"

"Your job for the day is finished. You can stay or go as you wish. I need to check on Nellie. Some of Belle's former patrons bring back memories."

Clara looked near the kitchen where Nellie had been standing to see the spot empty. "I'll leave you to it then."

Seeing that Becky was engaged in conversation, Clara set off for Mrs. Reese's house.

⬥

A tin of boot polish in hand, Lewis circled the mercantile again, keeping one eye on the view out the window. The sheriff's deputy crossed in front of the store on his way back to the jail. Lewis's plan to accidentally run into Clara had gone awry when the two cowboys tied their horses to the hitching post near Rose's Rescue. The men left several minutes ago in the direction of Lucky's Bar. Still Clara remained inside.

Philip Tarr came around the counter. "Sure I can't help you, Preacher? You're looking mighty lost."

"You know the feeling when you know you've forgotten something?" It was the closest thing to the truth he could say. One of the most difficult things Lewis faced as a minister was the inability to lie when a little white one would solve all of his problems.

"Considering you purchased boot polish last week, I think you're forgetting a heap of things."

"I did? Well, it won't hurt to have an extra tin." Lewis handed Phil the can and followed him to the counter.

"Five cents." Phil nodded to the window. "Looks like that new teacher is on her way home. Do you want me to add some lemon drops to your order so you have an excuse to talk with her?"

"Pardon?"

"You didn't think I believed you were interested in my soap display did you?"

Lewis took his purchase and hoped his cheeks weren't burning. "Thank you, Phil. Have a good afternoon."

The proprietor's laughter followed Lewis out of the store. So much for his perfectly timed exit. To catch up with Clara, he would have to run across the courthouse yard in the center of the town square.

Any number of parishioners could notice him if he were to race through the town running after Clara. Not the accidental meeting he'd planned. His chances of reaching her before she turned at the corner were close to nonexistent. Torn, Lewis waited for a wagon to pass before crossing the street to the courthouse. If he cut through the building, no one would see him running.

A man in a bowler hat stepped out of the post office and into Clara's path. The man removed his hat with a flourish. Lewis should have guessed he had competition. Fortunately, that distraction would give him the time he needed to intercept Clara. Using the cross pattern of the courthouse to his advantage, Lewis entered through the north door.

An old cowboy stood in front of the south courthouse door, gazing out of the window, his hand on the doorknob. Lewis slowed his step. The cowboy turned. "Looks like we have competition, Parson. Looky there, the doc just exited the boot and saddle shop."

The cowboy opened the door. "Mr. Collins just stopped his wagon with those kids of his."

Lewis allowed the door to close behind the cowboy.

Four other men were interested in Clara? Granted, Mr. Collins—desperate to find a mother for his children—had proposed to at least ten women since Lewis had arrived in town. He'd half expected the widower to call during yesterday's supper. The only man of the four worth his salt was Dr. Palmer. Judging that the doctor learned his trade in the recent war, he was too old for Clara.

Quick steps clicked along the imported marble tiles behind him. Lewis exited the building to avoid a conversation with whomever was drawing closer.

Clara smiled at the men, but took a tiny step back with each addition to their group. She turned slightly, and Lewis could no longer see her face. Bowler hat stepped closer. What was wrong with the men? Couldn't they see if she took another step backwards she'd be in danger of stepping off the boardwalk and toppling into the street? Mr. Collins crowded her from the left.

Lewis was halfway across the courthouse lawn before he realized he'd decided to save her. The old cowboy leaned forward.

"Stop!" The word escaped Lewis's lips a moment too late, and Clara stepped back.

Dr. Palmer reacted first, pulling Clara to him. Lewis stopped at the edge of the road to allow a freight wagon to pass. He waited only a moment for the worst of the dust to settle and rushed across the street.

Clara clung to the doctor's arm. Dr. Palmer said something Lewis couldn't hear over the rattling of the wagons. The old cowboy and the man with the bowler hat each stepped back, nodding a farewell before taking off in different directions. Mr. Collins continued his suit, only this time, when Clara tried to step back, the doctor was there.

"Good afternoon." Lewis's greeting was enough to cause everyone to pause at his arrival. Clara's pinched smile wasn't as welcoming as he'd hoped. Dr. Palmer nodded; he was unlikely to leave her side until time assured him that Clara suffered no distress from her near fall. Collins wouldn't leave until he proposed. The best way to extricate her would be to distract Collins.

"Ah, Mr. Collins, just the man I was looking for. I have a matter to discuss with you." Lewis propelled the man down the walk to his wagon. "I received a peculiar donation today that I thought might interest you."

Mr. Collins looked over his shoulder. Lewis also glanced back, sure that the man beside him focused on Clara, who walked in the opposite direction on Dr. Palmer's arm. At least she was free of the men who crowded her.

"This better be good, Preacher. You made me miss my chance with the new girl."

Lewis debated pointing out the obvious—that Mr. Collins had as much chance with Clara as a snowball in a Texas summer. Aware the Collins family missed church yesterday, Lewis took a different tact. "Missed you yesterday."

"The little one was poorly. Hard for a man to get anywhere with those three." As a newspaper man Mr. Collins lacked the polish one expected. "I asked her if she wanted to marry me, and she didn't answer."

"Have you been introduced?"

"I was meaning to introduce myself."

As were several other men. "Miss Taylor isn't used to men introducing themselves on the street." Or proposing for that matter. Even if he had on Saturday morning.

"Taylor? Isn't that the name of your bride? Do you mean to tell me—"

Either Collins had only heard part of the town gossip, or he hadn't made the connections. "I have been, as they say, jilted by Miss Taylor's sister. We have long been acquainted."

"Then you can introduce me."

Lewis peered in the saddle shop window, hiding his face from his parishioner. "My introduction would do little good. Miss Taylor is not—" He searched for a word that would discourage Mr. Collins without revealing too much. "I am not in her good graces."

Mr. Collins harrumphed and held out his hand palm up. "Well, get on with what you dragged me away for. What do you have to give me?"

Lewis took the boot polish from his pocket. "As I said, it was a rather peculiar donation."

"I don't have time to pay attention to my shoes. Not with three motherless kids."

"Keep it anyway. You never know when you may need to impress someone with shiny shoes."

"Do you think Miss Taylor likes shiny shoes?"

"I - I wouldn't know."

"I bet she does, being from Boston and all." Mr. Collins tossed the tin in the air and caught it. "Thanks, Preacher."

Lewis took solace in the fact that he had rescued Clara in the moment, hoping he hadn't created a greater problem.

⬦

Dr. Palmer stopped in front of Mrs. Reese's home. "I have other calls to make."

Clara let go of his arm. "Thank you for seeing me safely home. I hope I didn't keep you from your rounds."

"No need to apologize again. I'm more than glad you didn't become one of my patients." He tipped his hat and retraced his steps up the street.

The gate clicked shut behind her. Clara took one last look at the handsome doctor's retreating back. She guessed him to be ten years or more her senior—not ancient by any means. Clara believed his claim that his presence at the town square was circumstantial. He seemed far too busy to idle about in the heat waiting for her. As for the other men ... It seemed as if Becky's predictions of proposals were off by a day. Even Lewis had been there, although he had steered away the man that nearly forced her to step into the street after saying something about getting hitched.

Catherine would relish so much attention from the local bachelors. Clara sighed. She'd gone hours without thinking of her twin. Regrettably, she'd missed checking at the post office, although it was likely too early for news from her sister. What would Bernard's family think of the elopement? Would Catherine continue to pretend to be her? A throb in her temple reminded her to not contemplate the future, an action that could only lead to a headache.

Mrs. Reese sat on the horsehair sofa in the parlor with a book in her lap. "I wondered when you would come home. Are Nellie and Becky staying at the Rescue for dinner?"

Clara untied her hat and set it on a side table. "Yes, they said they would."

"Why didn't you?"

"I'm not sure of my place. At Bradford, our teachers never stayed to eat with us." Clara sat on the other end of the couch.

"Rose's is a far cry from Bradford. A Bradford education is a nicety where Rose's is a necessity."

Clara turned the words over in her mind. A woman could survive the modern world without knowledge of French or German or most other subjects taught at her alma mater. What could she teach the women at Rose's?

"I think I understand that from Emily's letters. I just feel so—" She let the words hang. "Like I don't belong. They are all friends. I'm—"

"Not a prostitute?"

Clara sucked in a breath. "No. I mean, I'm not, but I know they didn't have many choices. My life with its problems has been relatively perfect."

"Comparing burdens rarely works to anyone's advantage. In this past week, you have had some rather shocking turns of events. Just because they are not as dire doesn't mean they haven't given you some level of compassion."

"I am not sure I follow."

"Isn't one of the reasons you didn't return to Boston was that your sister left behind evidence that would ruin your reputation?"

Thoughts of her reputation and the difficulty of proving to her parents, which could take a few months, that her sister's letter was false, had crossed her mind. "That wasn't the primary reason."

"Still, you understand firsthand what it feels like to not want to face people from your past because of what they might think of you."

"I do, don't I? I hadn't thought of that."

"You have also been taken advantage of in different ways than some of them, but enough for you to know the pain of being forced into a situation beyond your control. While I wouldn't tell the women of the Rescue your experiences, lest they think you are trying to compare, you can use your experiences as seeds for your own empathy and feel like less of an outsider."

The kiss flashed through her mind. Perhaps some of them felt the same confusion when it came to men. While she was angry at Lewis for taking advantage, she admittedly thought of the moment because she had enjoyed kissing him. Thus, she had been in a quandary like no other—both hating and liking the experience at the same time. Could some of the women be of two minds about their experience? Perhaps happy that they had survived and hating themselves at the same time. "I see. There is really nothing preventing us from becoming friends is there?"

"There rarely is something that prevents two strangers from becoming friends other than their own distrusts and cautions." Mrs. Reese's smile seemed as full of wisdom as she did. "Now, how was your first day?"

"Odd. It isn't like any of the schools I've been to. I never imagined not giving marks or allowing students to come and go as they wish. Yet they seem eager to learn. Then, as the day ended, these two men burst in. Emily faced them down. Does that happen often?"

"Men looking for the former establishment?" Mrs. Reese didn't say brothel.

"Yes."

"Too often, as far as I am concerned. Neither Emily nor I thought of the possibility when we created Rose's. We repainted, put up a new sign, replaced the doors, added shutters, and still men walk in expecting to find the Bull's Eye. We have been looking at another property for Rose's, but neither Emily nor I have the funds. Between donations and the items the women sell, we hope to move next year."

"Why don't you keep the front door locked?"

Mrs. Reese set her book to the side. "Some of those women can't stand being locked in, even if they know all they have to do is throw the bolt to get out. Convincing them to allow the front doors to be locked at night is tough. Others wish to have every lock bolted to keep people out. It's an interesting balance with the bedrooms upstairs."

Clara didn't ask why. It was a question she didn't want an answer to as she'd learned from Emily's letters that her imagination couldn't begin to comprehend the terrors some people had to endure. "I noticed a boy sitting outside part of the day. When the men came in he ran for the sheriff. Who is he?"

"That is Donny. He keeps a lookout for trouble—one of his many jobs around town. He's still young enough that the women don't mind having him hang around."

"Oh, Emily wrote about him. She says she has to bribe him to go to school."

Mrs. Reese laughed. "The kid earns almost as much sitting in the schoolhouse in the winter as he does running errands in the summer. Doc is determined to see the boy through college."

"Some of the men's universities have running clubs. Donny would do well in them."

"Perhaps, but that is for him to decide when he is older." Mrs. Reese poured two tumblers full of lemonade from her ever-present pitcher. "Anything else happen today?"

Clara took the offered glass. "Not until I walked home. I wasn't accosted, exactly, but halfway through the square, men started coming from every direction trying to talk to me. Not one of them had been introduced to me. If it hadn't been for Dr. Palmer, I would have fallen off of the boardwalk."

"I wondered if that was him I saw through the window."

"He was kind enough to escort me home." Clara took a sip letting an ice chip float into her mouth. She played with it until it melted. "One of the men may have proposed. I didn't exactly understand what he said, so I didn't answer."

"Wise woman." Mrs. Reese set the glass down. "Was the preacher among them?"

"Lewis? No. At least, not at first. He came over as I was leaving and distracted the man who I think proposed to me." Clara pursed her lips. "I don't remember Lewis saying hello to me."

Perhaps Lewis had greeted her. She'd been so overwhelmed by all the attention that his addition to the group had been stressful. It quickly resolved into relief as his purpose seemed to be not to add to the situation as she feared he might.

"You think a man proposed?"

"I'm not sure. He said something about children and mother, but that is when I nearly stepped off the boardwalk and into the street."

"Ah, that must be Mr. Collins. He owns the newspaper. Emily found his way of courting difficult too. There is not a woman in the area over twenty he hasn't proposed to." Mrs. Reese's forehead scrunched. "Except for the women at Rose's."

"Becky warned me yesterday that I would receive proposals. I didn't believe her."

"Once, I received fifteen proposals in one afternoon. Most of the men didn't know my name. Of course I turned them down. I was much younger then, but I knew what love was and that I didn't need a man to survive. Nowadays, any proposal that comes is from a gold digger." Mrs. Reese shook her head and paused, lost in the memory. "There are women who would have accepted if only for a place to call home. For myself, I've only met two or three such women."

Questions about Mrs. Reese's past flooded Clara's mind. She only knew her landlady well enough to ask some of them. She needed wisdom and a guiding hand right now. "Why didn't you marry again?"

"Simple. A widow controls her own money and property; a wife can't. I never met a man whom I loved enough to gamble my security on him. I had love once, and I don't know how many women get that type of relationship twice."

"Oh." Clara wasn't sure what that meant for her. She'd thought herself in love once. She sipped her lemonade. Could she ever trust a man enough to give up the little freedom she had as a teacher? Probably. She didn't have enough money to last her more than a few weeks without a job.

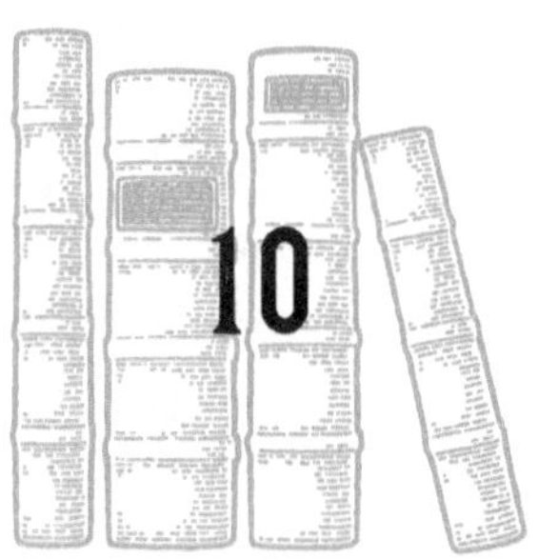

10

"I made Mama's lamb pie because she said you liked it so much. Aren't you going to try some?" A young woman in blue held out a platter expectantly. Most of the single women at the church social wore blue. Reportedly, it was his favorite color. How the congregation came to that conclusion, he wasn't sure. Blue was Clara's color, although tonight she wore a green dress.

Lewis spooned the smallest portion he could onto his plate. The girl's brow raised, and he added another half spoonful to his already overflowing plate. He smiled and muttered a thanks before stepping out of line. The mother of the next woman in line scowled at him. Lewis pointed to his plate. "I'll return when I lighten my load."

The woman's frown deepened. Perhaps he shouldn't have referred to his food as a load, a better word than burden. Lewis turned to the crowd filling the area in the shade of the church. He had not anticipated the number of families that reserved a space for him on their picnic blankets—most with daughters of marriageable or almost marriageable age. No matter where he sat, someone would be upset.

He also wouldn't have the opportunity to empty his plate by any means other than eating. Lewis hoped he had enough bicarbonate of soda to soothe the effects of the food he must consume. How was it that every choice he made related to his marriage, even a social, could turn to disaster so easily? He wandered toward the back of the church. Perhaps a visit to the privy might… No, there were too many eyes on him for such an obvious subterfuge to work.

Donny waved from his place near his sisters and widowed mother. Mrs. Owen left no extra space near her. She'd been extremely outspoken in her desire not to remarry and never left an opening for any man to get close to her. She would not welcome his intrusion.

Mr. Collins sat with his children and had left more than enough room for guests. The chances he would ask for an introduction to Clara were too high for Lewis to consider sitting with the family. His little Aubry wore a hand-me-down dress today, an action that should clear up the questions as to the gender of the child that had worn infant gowns for far too long.

Lewis searched for another safe place to sit. Mrs. Reese sat with Nellie, Becky, and a handful of the women from the Rescue. It was the first time for most of them to attend anything at the church. Clara was not among them. He meandered around the other groups and over to their place under a large tree.

"May I sit here?"

Several pairs of eyes turned to him and then to Mrs. Reese.

"Of course you may."

If his plate dropped as he sat down, he could avoid eating the preposterous amount of food he'd taken. Or not. Likely the mothers would come running to refill his plate, so he didn't miss out on their daughters' cooking. He sat carefully, not spilling a drop.

"That's a heap of food you got there."

"Becky." Mrs. Reese shook her head.

Lewis smiled at the girl. "The hazards of being a preacher. I can't politely turn anyone down. No one understands if I only take a teaspoonful of each item. When I am done, I'll need to go back as I haven't had any of Nellie's cake."

Nellie smiled or grimaced. Lewis was never sure until she spoke. "You'll have an ache as bad as if a mule kicked you before then. I won't be offended if you don't eat any tonight."

"Thank you, Nellie. As much as I love your cakes, I welcome the opportunity not to have to eat more this evening."

Miss Petunia snagged her son's foot, dragging him back across the blanket as he'd attempted to crawl off in a mad dash. "It seems to me that polite folks shouldn't be forcing you to eat so much."

Lewis took a bite of the lamb pie and immediately wished he'd tried the chicken first, as his teeth met with something roughly the texture of shoe leather.

Miss Lavender looked over her shoulder at the crowd. "It isn't polite folk, it's the marriage-minded mamas who want to snag a reverend for their daughters. You can feel them glaring, wondering why he would sit with the sinners."

Lewis swallowed the lump in his mouth. There wasn't enough bicarb in the entire town to solve the problems he would have tonight, however, he could set the women at ease. "Miss Lavender."

"Save it, Preacher. I know how you feel, as well as the good ones like Miss Emily and even your Miss Clara. You know as well as I do, these people will never accept us." Miss Lavender stood and brushed off her skirt.

"They won't ever accept you if you don't give them a chance." The words were out of his mouth before he could soften them.

Clara appeared next to Miss Lavender and linked a friendly arm through hers. "I've heard there is an amazing peach pie made by someone named Hannah. Would you mind pointing out the pie and the baker for me?"

Miss Lavender looked like she might bolt. Lewis said a quick prayer that she wouldn't. After a long moment, Miss Lavender nodded. "We'd better hurry. Her pies always go first."

Lewis watched them walk away as he stuffed a bite of chicken into his mouth. How had Clara known the right question to ask Miss Lavender to get her to stay? If Miss Lavender had left, the other women would have followed, destroying any headway they'd made into the community. When had Clara gotten the gumption to act that way? Intrepid was hardly a word he would have used to describe Clara in the past.

Mrs. Reese tapped him on the shoulder. "You should stop staring before others take notice."

Lewis looked at the plate in his hands. Mystery beef in sauce or some sort of beans?

"Reverend, would you mind getting a biscuit for Scotty?" Miss Petunia retained a hand on her son's foot. "We'll watch your plate."

A biscuit, just the thing to help the next items on his plate go down. "My pleasure. Does anyone else need something?"

The women shook their heads. Lewis hurried to the center of the food tables and found a biscuit as well as a fluffy roll that must have come from Hannah's kitchen. He plucked one from each platter and hurried back to the tree, avoiding more than making a few nods to his parishioners.

He returned to find a plate sitting in the same spot but empty of all but a few drops of gravy.

"Oh, Reverend, I am so sorry. Scotty got loose and knocked your plate into the dirt. We cleaned it up the best we could."

Miss Petunia's sly grin didn't match her penitent voice.

Lewis crouched down. "Well, Scotty, I am not in favor of rewarding poor behavior, but in this case, I think your mother should share the biscuit with you."

Miss Petunia took the offered biscuit. "My thoughts exactly."

Becky, Nellie, and Mrs. Reese all studied their plates intensely. Becky covered her mouth with her hand, her smile evident.

Lewis scooped up his plate. "Off to get round two."

He passed Miss Lavender and Clara on his way back to the food tables. Neither looked up at him, but he was quite sure he heard a giggle.

⟶◆⟵

"What is between you and the reverend?" Lavender led Clara the long way around the churchyard to their group, balancing two plates of pie in her hand.

Clara lifted her skirt an inch higher with her free hand to avoid catching it on the coarse weeds that passed for grass. "He is my older brother's best friend and our next-door neighbor. I've known him all my life."

"Is that all?"

"Well, he was engaged to my twin..."

"But you fancied him." Lavender stopped and looked Clara in the eye. "Don't deny it. I've seen you trying very hard not to look at him."

Unable to lie, Clara whispered. "I did."

"Not 'do'?"

"I'm not sure anymore. I'm beginning to wonder if I knew him as well as I thought I did."

"Do we ever know anyone else?" A sadness veiled Lavender's eyes.

"I thought so, but even my twin is a mystery to me. I spent most of my life within feet of her, still, she surprised me beyond measure." Clara watched her feet, not wanting Lavender to press her about Catherine.

"You have no idea what you are doing."

Taken aback, Clara stumbled a half step. "What do you mean?"

"You're lost like us. Every plan you ever made is gone, and you don't know what to do next."

"I suppose, in a way, yes. I know I am teaching. Other than that, everything else is a bit wobbly. You are rather perceptive."

Lavender sighed. "Four hundred and ninety-seven days taught me more than I ever want to know about reading people."

They'd reached the group, so Clara didn't answer. Lavender handed her extra plate to Petunia before sitting down. Clara took the empty space next to Lavender, who started eating. They abandoned the prior conversation for now.

Petunia broke off a piece of pie crust and gave it to her son who sat in her lap, tied in place with Petunia's apron. "Y'all missed my Scotty saving the preacher. Tipped his plate into the dirt, my boy did. Done me proud to see him do a good turn for another, bein' so young and all."

Becky laughed. "Nellie's hand may have helped out a bit."

Nellie crossed her arms and glared at her friend. "Preacher was going to make himself sick eating all of that. I can't stand seeing anyone eat food they don't like."

"He's been right kind to us. It was the least we could do," said Petunia.

Clara didn't hold back the giggle welling up inside. These women were remarkable.

The others joined in her laughter. Scotty looked from his mother to the other women as a smile grew on his face and he tipped back his head. A sound between a squeal and a giggle erupted from the boy, sending the women into another peal of laughter. As soon as the women stifled their giggles, Scotty started again. Having not spent much time around young children, the range of emotions shown by the boy surprised Clara. Up until now she'd assumed babies only cried and slept.

As another round of Scotty's giggles died, Lewis returned with a new plate of food. "Don't stop laughing on my account. You are the most jovial group here."

Miss Lavender looked around them. Clara did as well. A few people looked their way, some of them with disapproving frowns.

Mrs. Reese spoke softly. "Don't let those fuddy-duddies ruin our joy. Some of them don't remember what it is like to have a good laugh."

"They would laugh too, if they had a baby like Scotty," said Becky lightening the mood.

"Seeing all those dour faces, I may need to give a sermon on rejoicing," said Lewis.

"A sermon on being happy? Isn't that one of those oxymora-things Miss Emily taught us?" asked Rae.

"Oxymoron?" A smile returned to Lavender's face. "I do believe you may be correct. A joyful sermon could be a contradiction."

Lewis set his fork back on his plate. "What do you mean? I try to put joy and hope in all of my sermons."

"True, but I have never heard you preach on being joyful." Mrs. Reese's comment was met with several nodding heads.

"Well, then I have found the subject for next Sunday's sermon. I will prove that a sermon on joy is not an oxymoron."

"This may be worth going to the regular service to see the looks on people's faces," said Nellie.

"You are all welcome to come anytime."

No one immediately responded to Lewis's invitation. Clara suspected it wasn't the first time such an offer had been made.

Lavender broke the silence. "You know, ladies, it is high time that we start attending regular church. It would be a good thing for those folks to see that God's forgiveness works. Reverend Staples, you promise a sermon on joy, and I'll promise to come."

"Would my Scotty be welcome?" asked Petunia.

"Children are always welcome." The sincerity that radiated from Lewis was unmistakable. "If you'd rather not come though, I will repeat every word for you Sunday evening."

A couple of the women nodded. Around them, families started packing up their picnic things.

Mrs. Reese stood. "We should leave before the evening bugs find us. I have no intention of getting covered in bites."

Clara pitched in to gather the dinnerware and pack it into the basket.

"Miss Clara, can you hold Scotty for a moment? I need to use the necessary."

Clara held out her arms for the boy, and Petunia dashed off.

Scotty studied Clara solemnly. Did he know she'd never held a child before? The baby reached out his chubby hand and patted Clara's cheek and stared deep into her eyes. All her life, she'd been weighed against some standard or compared to her sister, but Scotty's intense gaze weighed and judged her against a scale with no definition. After a long moment, he smiled and bobbed his head before collapsing against her shoulder.

Clara adjusted her hold, afraid of dropping the boy if he moved suddenly.

"Reverend?" someone called.

Clara looked up to see if there was a problem. Lewis stood a few feet away, assessing her as Scotty had. Their eyes met, and something fluttered inside of Clara, a feeling reminiscent of their kiss. The person called again, and Lewis turned away.

Clara calmed her heart as her eyes followed him. Though different than in the novels, the feeling buzzing through her could only be attraction. How could she be drawn to Lewis when she was determined not to like him? Preposterous. There was no reason she should think of Lewis as anything other than a friend. If he even deserved that much from her.

Scotty shifted in her arms. Clara directed her attention to the baby. His eyes fluttered shut, and he relaxed. Clara rubbed his back and was rewarded with the tiniest of sighs.

"Well, I'll be." Petunia's exclamation was barely above a whisper. "He must like you to fall asleep like that. Would you mind carrying him back to Rose's? I don't want to wake him."

Clara nodded and joined the group walking back to their home. Scotty opened unseeing eyes when she stepped up onto the boardwalk. Once at Rose's, Clara followed Petunia up to her room. Lace curtains fluttered in the breeze coming through the screened window. The room, painted in pale blue, was bright and cheerful. Petunia helped Clara lay Scotty in a crib, then motioned her out into the hall.

"Thank you for your help. I'm glad Scotty likes you. I wasn't too sure at first about you—I thought you might think you were better than us—but you just don't like talking much, do you?"

"My sister always talked so much, I didn't need to. I'm sorry if you thought…" Unsure what word to use, Clara allowed the sentence to trail off.

Petunia gave Clara a quick hug. Clara returned the unexpected sign of acceptance.

"You better hurry home. The sun is going to set, and it isn't always safe to walk home in the dark." An ominous tone laced Petunia's words as she walked to the stairway.

Clara suppressed a shudder.

Lavender stood on the landing. "Looks like the preacher is waiting to walk you home. Another bloke is out there. Avoid him."

"Why would Lewis be waiting for me?" Clara didn't realize she'd spoken the words out loud until Lavender answered.

"Because he fancies you."

"No, he doesn't." He couldn't. Clara couldn't let him.

Lavender raised her brows. "I know when a man fancies a woman. I saw the way he looked at you when you were holding Scotty. He wasn't the only one."

Clara tried to get a better look out of the front window. From this angle, she could only see legs. A third man joined the other two.

Standing two stairs below Clara, Lavender bent for a better view. She frowned. "Trust me, your best choice for an escort home is the preacher. I'm going to go down and lock the door after you."

Clara followed Lavender down the stairs. Three men. Only the most popular girls at Bradford ever had that many beaus hanging around.

———⟫◆⟪———

Lewis forced a smile as he extended his hand, first, to the man who joined him, and then to Mr. Collins who stood on the boardwalk outside the Rescue. Mr. Collins's children sat in the back of the wagon only a few feet away.

The door behind him opened, and Clara stepped out. "Thank you so much for waiting, Reverend."

He did his best to mask his surprise at her declaration as she tucked her hand into the crook of his elbow. "No problem at all."

Once at his side, she looked up to acknowledge the others around her.

The last man to arrive tipped his hat. "Have a good evening, Preacher, Miss."

Mr. Collins moved into Lewis's path. "You said you'd introduce us."

With no gracious way out, Lewis turned to Clara. "Miss Taylor, this is Mr. Collins. He runs the newspaper. His children are sitting over there in the wagon."

"Nice to meet you, Mr. Collins." Clara didn't extend her hand. Instead her grip tightened on Lewis's arm.

"I have my wagon, if you want to ride."

"Thank you, no. Reverend Staples has already offered to escort me."

Mr. Collins opened his mouth and then shut it. A wise move. Lewis was sure the next words out of the man's mouth would be to point out he had polished his shoes.

This was the time to make their escape. Lewis nodded in Collins's direction and waved to the children. "Good evening, children."

"Good night, Reverend!" They waved back. Their father had no choice but to join them.

Once his competition was gone, Lewis escorted Clara down the boardwalk.

"I hope you forgive my presumption that you were waiting for me."

"Nothing to forgive. I was waiting for you. I didn't want you walking home alone. How are you settling in?"

"Well enough. I think it is going to take me some time to get used to the Texas heat. I thought summer in Boston was hot…"

"I did too."

"The shade isn't much cooler. No matter how many times I think the shade of a tree will give some respite, it doesn't." After they crossed a street, Clara loosened her grip on his arm but kept her hand resting there.

Her touch warmed him in a way that had nothing to do with the weather. "How is working at the Rescue?"

"I've only taught for three days. I think I am settling in. It is not the classroom situation I am used to."

"I imagine not."

"This afternoon, I sat with a woman as she read *Jane Eyre* to me. She wanted me to correct her speech as she wishes to speak more ladylike."

"Then she has a good teacher." The compliment slipped out easily. Of course he'd never witnessed Clara teaching, but she'd showed an incredible amount of patience over the years, a quality which all good teachers needed.

"I am not so sure. I love the slower speech of the South and hope she doesn't lose it entirely trying to change everything about her."

"I'm sure she'll find her way."

"When Emily told me she didn't use marks or a grading system, I wondered how I would motivate the students. Motivation is not a problem; trying to learn everything at once is."

"I remember a little girl who wanted to know everything. She'd follow her brother and me all over, asking us questions."

"You would tell fibs to me."

"Fantastical stories." Now was not the time for her to remember all of his follies and foibles.

"Lies." Her soft smile showed she wasn't upset.

"Not exactly. I had no idea the answer to some of your questions. Like where the butterflies went."

"They don't turn into fairies. I spent hours trying to catch one just to see. Then it died."

"I helped you give it a funeral."

"You even provided the matchbox, as I recall."

"It was the least I could do. The only thing worse than all of your questions was when you cried." Thankfully that had not been often that he could recall.

"I always cry at funerals. It is the proper thing to do."

"So it is." They turned on to the street where Mrs. Reese's house stood. Only a precious few minutes remained in their conversation. He slowed his steps. "I handled things poorly the other night. I have given you no reason to want to be in my company. Still, I would consider it the highest honor if you would allow me to call on you properly."

Clara turned her attention to the picket fence.

Two, three, four. Lewis counted their steps as he waited for her answer.

She stopped and turned to him. "What is your intention?"

The question was one he would expect a father to ask. Lewis swallowed. "I intend to see if we suit, if our friendship will bloom into more."

Her head tilted as she peered up at him. "You intend to propose?"

"Eventually."

"Why?"

Lewis couldn't help smiling. "Because I once wished on a butterfly…"

Clara's hand slipped from his arm and perched on her hip. "Lewis Staples. This is a serious question."

Immediately he missed her touch. "And it deserves a serious answer. Because I made the biggest mistake of my life last year, and I want to set everything right."

To his surprise Clara frowned. What had he said wrong?

A sigh escaped her lips before she answered. "You are welcome to call, but I am not going to turn away other callers either."

The answer was better than a refusal. "A week from Friday night a violinist will be playing at the theater. Will you come with me?"

"I've seen the posters, and I do miss music. I'll attend with you…" Clara looked at her hands.

Her answer left an unsaid condition. "But?"

"You don't propose or speak of marriage."

The entire point of courting a woman was to convince her to marry.

Clara laid her hand back on his arm. "Agreed?"

"I won't propose or speak of marriage." *For now.* Clara would come around eventually. He hoped.

11

Rose's Rescue didn't hold classes on Friday or Saturday. Still, Clara went both days. They'd spent much of Friday completing orders for a Fort Worth dress shop and sorting various handmade items and baked goods to sell at the local outdoor market.

Saturday morning, Clara arrived with Becky as the sun broke over the eastern horizon. Sheriff Morgan leaned against the post nearest the front door. He straightened as they neared. "Mornin', ladies."

"Is something wrong?" asked Becky.

"I wish folks would stop thinking there was something wrong when they see me." The sheriff's frown only lasted a moment.

Clara shifted the basket she carried to her other arm. "It is a natural assumption. You were standing outside of Rose's early in the morning."

The sheriff rubbed the back of his neck. "Emily is feeling a mite poorly this morning and sent me to ask if Miss Clara would go in her place to Fort Worth with Miss Lavender."

"I knew something was wrong," muttered Becky.

Images of drunkards and men shooting at each other filled Clara's mind. Only yesterday after hearing some of the women's stories she'd decided not to venture to any town that designated part of it as Hell's Half Acre. Yet Lavender could not travel to Fort Worth alone, and most of the other women didn't dare go near the town. If someone didn't go, they might lose the contract with the dress shop.

Likely, Lewis would be at the local market hoping to speak with her. Ever since he walked her home Wednesday night, she'd avoided him—not an easy feat, given that he loitered around the square each afternoon about the time school ended. Clara took a deep breath. This wasn't about avoiding Lewis. The women needed help. "I'd be glad to."

The sheriff's mouth broke into a wide grin. "Emily will be so relieved. Have a safe trip."

Becky stared after the sheriff as he jogged down the steps and across the courthouse lawn. "See? Trouble. Now you won't be at the market with us."

"Emily must have thought you could survive without me."

"But there was so much I wanted to show you."

Clara opened the door. "And there will be other days."

They stepped into the building only to be engulfed in last-moment preparations. If Becky answered, the commotion from every corner of the room drowned out her voice.

"Which crate has the—?"

"Where is the—?"

"Scotty, let go of Mama's hair." Petunia's was the only statement she could unravel from the rest of the bustle.

Lavender set three hat boxes on the table. "Oh, good, you're here. I saw you got the message about Emily. Donny will be here with the wagon to take us to the depot any moment."

"Is he old enough to drive a wagon?" The boy couldn't be even twelve yet.

"His mother's mules are so old and slow, we don't worry about them running off."

"I've never seen mules pull a wagon, only read about them."

Lavender pointed out the window. "Now you've seen it. Let's hurry. We don't want to miss the train."

A whirlwind of activity filled the next half hour. Clara struggled to catch her breath when she finally settled into her seat on the train. "Is it always like this?"

Lavender fanned her face. "Unfortunately, yes. Doesn't matter how well we plan, something extra happens. I had no idea that Morning Glory turned milliner—hence, the extra hatboxes. I hope they sell. I don't want to cart a half dozen hats back."

Six hat boxes surrounded Clara and Lavender. Clara wasn't sure how she got her three onto the train without dropping or squishing one. Donny's help with the crates going in the luggage car had been invaluable. "How are we going to carry all this stuff when we get to Fort Worth?"

"We hired a teamster with a wagon for the day. Don't worry, he's a friend of TJ's family. We use the same one every time."

"Did I look worried?" asked Clara.

"I'm afraid they told you too many stories about Fort Worth. You need to understand that the tales we tell about the marksmen or stampeding cattle, is more so we don't think about the life we had in Fort Worth or wherever we were. We don't talk about our former jobs much."

"Did you live in Fort Worth?" Clara wondered how Lavender had ended up in Texas. Philadelphia was almost as far as Boston.

"No. That is why I'm the one who comes here. None of us wants to be recognized, and I have the least chance."

Clara nodded. "I could see where that would be awkward."

"I'm sure I will run into someone from one of my pasts someday. I pray every morning that it won't be today."

"May I ask what you mean by one of your pasts?"

"I've lived three lives under three different names. The one before, the one during, and the one after. I'd hate either of my pasts to find me." Lavender opened an issue of *Harper's Bazaar* she received in the mail yesterday, ending the conversation.

Clara watched out the window, wishing she'd brought something to read. There were few people from her life she wished to avoid. Bernard. She had no desire to see him ever again, although if she were to visit Catherine, it would be inevitable. Any day now, she should get a letter from her sister or mother. Likely, it would take several letters to her mother before any confusion was sorted. She'd half expected a telegram to either her or Lewis to confirm which daughter was in Texas and which had eloped. Lewis's letter must have been enough to pacify Father. Hopefully, he had done nothing ridiculous like asking for her hand. Wouldn't that be a fine mess?

"I said, what do you think of this pattern?" Lavender pointed to an illustration of lace edging.

"It is very nice."

Lavender set the magazine into her lap. "What were you pondering so intently? I asked you the question three times. Starting with, 'Isn't this rather bland?'"

"Oh, I'm sorry. I didn't mean to ignore you."

"Is it the preacher?"

"What do you mean?"

"What were you thinking of?"

"In a way. I was thinking of my sister and my parents and how complicated things have become."

"He proposed to you, didn't he? Same as all those other desperate men."

"I wouldn't say he was desperate. Unlike the other proposal I received this week, Lewis knows me."

"Why did you turn him down? His eyes don't wander like other men's. Before he arrived, Reverend Green had a junior minister ..., well, his eyes wandered." Lavender made a face. "Reverend Staples will do right by whomever he marries."

"I want Lewis to want to marry me, but not just as a fill in for my missing sister. Or to fill a spot as the wife he needs. Just because we look alike doesn't mean my twin and I are interchangeable. I want a man to marry me for me." The words sounded funny all together. Clara wasn't sure how to better explain what she felt.

"Good for you. Most women wouldn't pass on a proposal if the man had a thimbleful of decency in him."

This conversation needed to end before it went much further. Clara wasn't ready to discuss her situation with Lewis. "Would you turn down a proposal from a decent man?"

"That's different. I'm not the kind of woman a decent man should marry. Imagine what would happen if people discovered my past." Lavender opened her magazine and turned the pages.

Had their friendship progressed to where Clara could ask a question? "So you have turned down someone?"

Lavender's brows pinched together. "How did we start discussing me? I thought I was telling you not to let the preacher get away."

The train whistle blew and the conductor announced the next stop as Fort Worth. Lavender tucked her magazine away, and Clara tucked her thoughts of Lewis deep where no one could see them.

⟛⬦⟚

Lewis wandered around the outdoor market a second time. Having already purchased more vegetables than Reverend Green and he could eat in a month, he was running out of excuses to be about. The Rescue's stall featured lace-edged handkerchiefs, knit baby socks, aprons, and other clothing items intended to entice the womenfolk. Lewis couldn't remain at it long without raising suspicions. Nellie and Becky sat at a separate table selling baked goods. The chances they would tell Clara he inquired about her were high but worth the risk.

"Morning, ladies."

"Hello, Reverend. Care for some rolls? They are from a new recipe Miss Clara brought with her." Becky pointed to a basket of Parker House rolls that looked like those his mother's cook baked each week for Sunday dinner.

There couldn't have been a more natural opening. "A half-dozen please. Isn't Miss Clara here this morning?"

Nellie wrapped the rolls in paper. "She took Miss Emily's place and went to Fort Worth with Lavender."

Lewis dropped his coins into Becky's palm and added the rolls to his sack of vegetables.

Nellie leaned over the table. "Aren't people feeding you anymore? That is a heap of food for two preachers."

"Nellie, we are not supposed to pry." Becky's not so quiet whisper was met with a scowl.

"I ain't prying. Just observing." Nellie crossed her arms.

Lewis opened his sack again. "You are correct, I overbought. Do you think you could use squash and corn? I'll trade you for one of your little jumble cakes."

Nellie eyed him. "I suppose we could. We'd be getting the better deal. You'd better take four. Reverend Green has a fondness for them."

Lewis completed the trade and went on his way, suppressing the temptation to eat one of Nellie's jumbles as he walked. The knowledge that the thin wafer would leave crumbs on his black coat deterred him. As he was leaving, he spotted the Collins boy selling the Saturday edition *Hiramsville*

Times. Reverend Green enjoyed reading the news. "Anything good in there?"

The boy moved his hand to cover one of the headlines. "I don't know as you would like it much, preacher."

"Why not?"

"Someone wrote…" The tips of the boy's ears reddened. "They said some not nice things about you."

"Not to worry about it. If everyone had a good opinion of me, I wouldn't be doing my job." Lewis parted with his last two pennies.

The boy brightened and handed over the paper. "Thank you, and don't pay the letter any mind."

On the long walk home, he flipped the folded paper over to read. The first article was about a two-headed chicken being shown in Sherman. While an oddity, it was hardly enough to write about. The next article was about a shooting on the other side of Dallas. Lewis flipped the paper again only to move from news around the state, to corn and cotton prices. As curious as Lewis was about what might offend him, he couldn't balance his purchases and read the paper at the same time. A proper reading would require two hands.

Reverend Green looked up from his seat at the kitchen table when Lewis walked in. "Looks like you got more than carrots."

"I may have overestimated our need of beans and peas."

The Reverend slipped a paper to mark his place into the large commentary he was reading and closed the book. "Or you were unsuccessful in your search for Miss Taylor."

"What?" How had Reverend Green known of his intentions? Lewis was sure he hadn't announced them.

"You were gone longer than it takes to purchase a few vegetables and too short of a time to have a conversation with your girl."

"I don't have a girl."

"Obviously, if you can't even go talk to her."

"If you must know, she went to Fort Worth." Lewis put the rolls in the cupboard for later with three of the jumble cakes. He put the other one on a plate. "She's going out of her way to avoid me."

"If you intend on marrying her, you better find a way to get in her good graces sooner than later."

"Maybe I was right last year, and it really isn't God's will that I marry Clara, even if Catherine is beyond me now too."

Reverend Green pointed to the seat across from him. "You keep using that phrase, 'God's will,' as if it absolves you of your own choices."

"But when he leaves me with no choice, then what else can it be?"

Reverend Green sighed. "When were you left with no choices?"

"Last summer, when I proposed to Catherine thinking she was Clara."

Reverend Green held up both hands. "Stop. You chose not to correct the error."

"But Clara saw me kiss Catherine."

"Which, when explained, could have been forgiven. Assuming your guess was correct, and Catherine was trying to fool you into believing she was Clara, then there is no reason that her family would not have understood."

"But I'd been praying, and I told the Lord to give me a sign if I was choosing wrong."

"Of all the blockheaded..." Reverend Green thumped his book closed. "Do you even read the same Bible that I do? Asking God for a sign doesn't usually work out well."

"So what should I do?"

"It sounds to me like the first thing you need to do is stop leaving the choices up to chance. Decide if you really want to have Clara as your lifelong companion."

"I do." The wording of his answer being so close to the answers during a marriage ceremony caused Lewis to pause.

"Then the next thing is you better do something about it."

"What if it isn't what God…" Lewis trailed off under the intensity of the older reverend's glare.

"Before you say that phrase again, I want you to find it for me in the Bible and where it says to use it in the way you have been."

Lewis strode to the parlor and picked up the Bible on the side table. He thumbed through the pages, not sure where to find the passage.

"And so help me, if you claim it must be God's will that you marry her because she came here…" Green followed Lewis into the parlor. The exertion left him breathing hard. He waved at the book in Lewis's hands. "I'll save us both some time. Not once in all my years have I seen the phrase, 'God's will,' in the Good Book the way you are using it."

"But I've heard it all my life."

"No doubt from well-meaning people when a child dies, or when a storm kills someone, or some other tragic event for which we don't have an adequate explanation for." He paused to cough. "You think it is God's will that someone gets murdered or lies?"

"No."

"Of course not. That is why He gave us commandments and asked that we keep them. Keeping the commandments and loving our neighbors. That is God's will." Reverend Green spasmed as he coughed repeatedly. Blood stained his handkerchief. "Own up to your mistakes. I can't stand it when a man uses his religion to cover his own stupidity, especially if that man is a man of the cloth."

Lewis stared at his pale friend, more immediate concerns filling his mind. "Do I need to fetch the doctor?"

"Not much he can do about this. I just need some rest." Reverend Green shuffled off to his room.

The reverend's words tumbled in Lewis's mind like the sea during a storm. Everything couldn't be blamed on God. He'd known the second Catherine's lips touched his that something was wrong. He could have jumped away or anything else rather than kiss her back—an action he couldn't fully explain to himself and blamed on his nervousness. The other kisses he'd shared with Catherine had left him hollow. Those had been actions he performed because they were engaged. Lewis's heart had felt incomplete from that first, fateful kiss. He'd tried to explain to Clara, yet she hadn't accepted his proposal.

Lewis returned to the kitchen and put the vegetables in the bin. After removing his coat, he went to the table to read the newspaper as he ate one of the jumbles.

He flattened the crumpled newspaper, a single sheet folded to create four pages. On the back page, he found the article the Collins boy tried to hide.

⟣⟢

OUTRAGE IN HIRAMSVILLE AS DESPICABLE BLIGHT ON TOWN CONTINUES

After almost a year of operation, the building formerly known as the Bull's Eye, or simply Belle's, continues to bring undesirables to Hiramsville. This past Monday, the residents of the reformatory once again called on the sheriff's office when former clients appeared and demanded services from the ladies of the Rescue. On the 4th of July, many townspeople witnessed a woman clad in barely more than her underthings and an excess of rouge stumble into town to be taken in by the Rescue.

Now these women have the audacity to attend
Wednesday's Church gathering and were
welcomed by our jilted pastor. The congregation of faithful men and women were shocked
to find their unmarried pastor inviting them in!
It appears that the pastor is more interested in
finding a wife from among these fallen women
than he is with his flock, bypassing our fair and
virtuous daughters to sit on the same blanket as
a child of sin. Even the most desperate of Hiramsville's upstanding bachelors among us have not
stooped to such depths.

Each day on the way to the mercantile, the
post office, or the booksellers, our children are
subjected to walking by Rose's which, despite its
name change and new coat of paint, continues to
house the same women who made the building
a den of iniquity.

The good people of this churchgoing town are
calling on the Rescue to be removed. They do not
wish for its blight to remain beneath the shadow
of our new courthouse.

Signed, Upstanding Members of Hiramsville

The words felt like a sharp blade slicing his heart in two.
How could anyone in his congregation pen such a cruel
letter? Scotty was no more a child of sin than any other
child. Lewis had baptized him at Petunia's request, and many
of the congregation had reached out to the young mother
with gifts for her son.

The jumble cake no longer tempted him. He set it back
on the plate. He knew some of the parishioners held differ-
ing opinions about Rose's Rescue, and a few even stopped
donating to the church, lest the money support the Rescue.
But he'd never imagined anyone would demand the Rescue
leave town.

He stood from the table and paced around the kitchen, pondering what course of action he should take next. If he had not already planned the promised sermon on joy, he would be tempted to preach fire and brimstone tomorrow.

The silk fan did little to circulate the air inside of the chapel. Clara waved hers in time with the dozens of other women as Lewis continued to talk of joy. After hearing of yesterday's newspaper article, Clara assumed Lewis would change his sermon's subject. Instead, he kept his promise to the women of Rose's Rescue. More than half of them sat in the pews today. While there had been a few looks of disdain, some people went out of their way to greet the women before the service started. Not everyone agreed with the article

"And again in Psalms thirty-five, we read 'And my soul shall be joyful in the Lord.' What does that mean? Should we only be joyful in good times or should we find joy when life is bleak?" Lewis brought his sermon to an end with another question. "Have you ever told the Lord in prayer all the things that bring you joy? A tall tree, a spice cake, the smile of a child?"

No, thought Clara. Did people pray about things like that? Maybe ministers did. Although most she had ever heard pray gave long-winded sermons disguised as prayers. Clara couldn't fault Lewis for keeping his word. The sermon even gave her more points to ponder than one of the expected ones on sinning.

She was still thinking about things that brought her joy when people around her began to move toward the exit. Clara hoped she'd bowed her head for the benedictory prayer she couldn't recall hearing.

"Guess I'll be making the preacher's favorite pie for after our services tonight," said Nellie with a sigh. "I didn't think he could preach a sermon on joy, especially after yesterday's paper."

"I'm surprised he didn't mention anything about it," said Clara.

"Mama told me that sometimes it is best to act as if no one commented at all." Nellie touched the scarring on her cheek.

Mrs. Reese used her fan to direct them towards the door. "Whoever wrote that article will spend more time stewing about why nothing was said than you all did worrying if you should come today."

The heat outside the building was just as bad as it had been inside.

"Joy is hard to think about when it is hot as—" Becky stopped her sentence under Mrs. Reese's reproachful eye. "The thermometer at the bank registered 101 degrees yesterday. It is hot as that place."

"I wouldn't know. I've never been there." Mrs. Reese's comment garnered a few laughs.

"I'm glad I planned a cold supper for today. No sense in standing over a hot stove." Nellie's face fell. "I forgot I have to make a pie."

"What if you all come over and we make ice cream?" Everyone approved of Mrs. Reese's suggestion. "I'm sure the reverend will find it a perfect substitute for pie."

Clara followed the group to the edge of the churchyard. Dr. Palmer stood near his buggy. "Miss Clara, would you do me the honor of allowing me to escort you home?"

Tamping down her surprise, Clara nodded. The doctor was too old for her, wasn't he? Not old enough to be her father, certainly. He hadn't struck her as one of the men interested in marrying her the other day when he'd saved her from falling. He handed her up into his buggy. Clara arranged her skirt to give him plenty of room as he came around the other side and climbed up.

"I don't usually have my carriage at church, but I had a call to make this morning and missed half the meeting."

They quickly passed Mrs. Reese and the rest of those walking home from church.

"It feels awkward receiving a ride when Mrs. Reese is walking."

"If I offered her a ride, she would have chastised me with a lecture about her health."

"Yes, I can see how she might be affronted."

"How many proposals have you received this week?"

The question caught Clara so off guard she answered. "None after you saved me from falling off the boardwalk."

"I must say, I am surprised there haven't been more." The doctor's deep voice only had a bit of drawl to it.

"Are conversations always so blunt in the West?"

"A man just likes to know where he stands before he asks a woman if he may call on her."

Call on her? He gave no sign that he was joking.

"You wish to call on me?" Her voice squeaked on the last word.

"Only if it is acceptable."

How was she supposed to answer? Although she'd told Lewis she would accept other callers, she hadn't thought the possibility that two men would want to call on her existed.

Clara ran her finger along the ivory handle of her fan. "I have had another man ask to call on me. I told him I would accept other callers too."

"Fair enough. Do you know when he intends to call? I would not want to make the situation awkward for you."

"The only definite plans he has made with me are for Friday."

"The violinist? Don't answer that, it was rude of me to ask." The doctor stopped his buggy in the shade of a tree in front of Mrs. Reese's home. Instead of getting down, he turned to face her. "Would you accompany me on a ride by the river this evening? It should be cooler then."

"Yes, I will."

"I should warn you that interruptions in my profession happen often. Although I have no reason to expect one today, I will send word if I am kept away."

"Are you the town's only doctor?"

"I am now."

"Then I forgive you in advance if you cannot keep your appointments."

"I thank you for your understanding." Dr. Palmer got down from the carriage and came around to assist Clara. So short was the walk from the church that Mrs. Reese met them at the door.

"Did Clara invite you to come back for ice cream this afternoon?"

Clara's face burned. "No I didn't, I wasn't aware…"

"Sorry, dear. You must have left us before we finalized our plans." Mrs. Reese patted Clara's arm. "You are welcome to come, Doctor. We should be done at six and the reverend will give his Sunday night sermon to the Rescue in my backyard."

"If Miss Clara does not object, I will be here."

Lewis and the doctor in the same place? Yet she couldn't overturn Mrs. Reese's invitation. "Sounds lovely. I hope you can come."

"Six you say?" He looked to Mrs. Reese for confirmation. "Until then."

Clara watched him return to his buggy. No hitch slowed his step. He may be older, but certainly not old.

⋯⋯⋯

Lewis whistled as he strolled up to Mrs. Reese's house for the impromptu party. He rounded the corner and his heart sank. Clara stood on the porch, her eyes locked on the doctor's. The tune on Lewis's lips died as Clara's laughter filled the air.

A pang of jealousy twisted Lewis's gut. Hardly the feeling a minister should have an hour before his sermon. Lewis pushed away the envy he felt towards this man who captivated Clara's attention.

Out of all the men in town, Dr. Palmer was the one he trusted the most to be honorable in his intentions. He had earned the trust of the women of the Rescue. Not an easy feat. If Lewis was to face an opponent for Clara, the doctor was a worthy one.

Turning onto the walkway leading to the house, Lewis smiled as he did whenever meeting members of his congregation. "Good evening, Doctor. I'm glad you can join us."

"The offer of ice cream was too good to pass up. Since I missed most of your sermon this morning, I have the rare opportunity to hear it in full." Dr. Palmer shook Lewis's hand in greeting. "I have yet to figure out why babies insist on coming into the world early on Sunday mornings. I have missed half your sermons since you arrived."

Lewis hadn't heard of a new birth in the congregation, however he knew the doctor wouldn't tell him the identity of the parents without permission.

"Mrs. Reese had us set up chairs in the backyard. I believe everyone else is here." Clara led the men around the porch.

She hadn't taken the doctor's arm. That was a good sign, wasn't it?

The women from the Rescue mingled about the backyard under the shade of the trees. TJ sat on the bottom step cranking the handle of the ice cream maker. "The reinforcements are here. Just in time, gentlemen. Another minute and my shooting arm would have been out of commission."

"I hope not. Shoulder injuries are difficult to mend," said Dr. Palmer.

Lewis stepped over to take TJ's place. "Then I'll take my turn first. Preachers don't need their shoulders like sheriffs and doctors do."

TJ stood. "I'll go get more ice. It is close to being done, but the ice is melting fast, even in the shade."

Clara picked up the empty ice bucket. "I'll get the ice, sheriff. You deserve a rest."

"I'll help you, Miss Clara." Dr. Palmer followed her to the cellar door.

Lewis cranked harder. He'd been in Mrs. Reese's cellar a time or two. Built into one of the natural caves below the town, it stayed cool and covered an area as big as the house. On a day like this, he wouldn't want to come out. Especially if he was down there with a woman he was courting. One, two, … fifty. He counted the rotations of the crank to distract himself. Each crank became more difficult. Around the three hundred and twenty-second or so crank—he'd lost track—Clara and the doctor returned with more ice, which they added to the ice cream machine's bucket.

"That should do it. It is getting harder to turn. Another five minutes or so should finish it," said Lewis.

Dr. Palmer lifted the quarter-full bucket. "I'll take the rest of the ice inside so Thelma can add it to the lemonade. I haven't seen her since she returned. I must ask her how she liked the ocean."

Mrs. Reese came over to check on the progress of the ice cream. "Shall I make them wait until after your sermon to partake?"

"I don't see any reason why they can't eat it during. What better joy is there to have than a cooling dessert during a dry lecture?"

"It wasn't dry this morning."

"Good to hear. I wasn't sure if the long looks on some of the faces in the congregation were from the heat, my speaking, or some other cause."

"The newspaper perhaps? I could have done with a bit of fire and brimstone this morning. Whoever wrote that needs to be horsewhipped." Mrs. Reese punctuated her sentence with a jerk of her hand mimicking the action of swinging a whip.

"I would prefer they spend more time with their Bibles. I am of the opinion that all of us need more understanding." Reverend Green joined them. Apparently the lure of ice cream won out over the book he'd been studying when Lewis left. "From the look on your face, young man, I believe I timed my arrival perfectly."

Lewis stopped churning and cleared the brine off the lid before checking the ice cream. "It looks finished to me. What do you think, Mrs. Reese?"

She nodded and turned to the women. "Becky and Nellie, will you get the bowls?"

The only problem with allowing the others to eat during his sermon was that Lewis was forced to watch them. Knowing that a bowl had been set aside down in the ice cave was of little comfort. However, unlike that morning, every face was smiling.

At the conclusion of the sermon, Nellie brought him his bowl. "I liked the sermon today, both times. What are you going to speak about next week?"

"I'm not sure yet." The first bite of the cold, creamy peach ice cream ended with the anticipated wincing pain in his forehead.

"Are you going to talk about the newspaper article?" asked Rae.

"It depends. So far, no one has had the courage to speak to me yet. We have always known not everyone approves of the Rescue. Since they have vented their spleen in the paper, they may now be content," said Lewis.

"What is a spleen?" asked Petunia.

"It is an organ of your body, located about here." The doctor pointed to his left abdomen. "Years ago, physicians incorrectly thought that the spleen was responsible for making people angry because of a bile it produces. So to vent one's spleen meant that someone was getting rid of their anger."

"So the spleen doesn't make us angry?" asked Becky.

"No, it doesn't. Modern medicine believes it keeps us well. Now if you will excuse me, I promised Miss Clara a ride along the river."

Lewis watched in dismay as Clara crossed the lawn on the doctor's arm. He'd hoped to entice her on a sunset walk after the meeting. Now it seemed his only course of action was to wait for another opportunity.

"Reverend, your ice cream is melting." Miss Lavender's observation was entirely true.

Lewis plastered on a smile as he devoured the cold concoction, despite its soupy texture.

"A bit of advice. If you are going to court Clara, you need to try harder. Whatever memories you shared will not be enough." With that, Miss Lavender walked away, leaving Lewis alone.

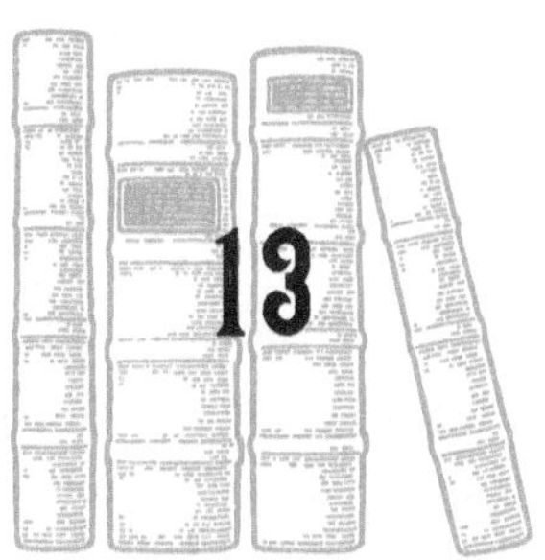

The clanking of a pan awoke Lewis. Another clunk caused him to sit up. The sun cast bright light into his room. He'd overslept. He pulled on his pants and shirt and rushed downstairs.

Reverend Green sat at the kitchen table innocently drinking a cup of coffee. The frying pans sat next to him. "About time you woke up."

"It seemed I had a bit of help this morning. Did you need me to make anything? An egg?"

"Eggs would be nice. I've already eaten the last of the bread. I left the last roll for you."

Lewis took the bowl of eggs from the shelf. "If you weren't a fellow man of the cloth, I'd call you a sneaky old man."

"I am what I am. Being a preacher for the last fifty years doesn't make me a saint." Reverend Green sipped his coffee and made a face. "It also doesn't make me a good cook. We are all human, Lewis. Something best kept in mind when others forget."

The lard Lewis dropped in the frying pan sizzled. He broke the eggs into the pan. He didn't bother asking Reverend

Green how he wanted them, as he'd learned last fall when he first arrived that anything other than burned satisfied his friend. "We aren't usually out of bread on a Monday morning. I must not be purchasing enough now that you are living here."

"Or not as many baked goods have been donated in the last few days."

There had been a decline in food since Wednesday's church picnic. "Maybe the women folk aren't cooking as much in the heat." Lewis flipped the eggs over.

"Their families still have to eat. I think it has more to do with the sentiment behind the news article. The food donations increased when you first arrived, and dropped after we announced you were engaged."

"So the baked goods are linked to my status as a single minister?"

"Young, single minister. I only received a loaf of bread here and there after my wife died."

Lewis scooped the eggs onto two plates. "So when I get married, I shouldn't expect any more food from the congregation."

"Eggs, uncooked meat, and vegetables. An invitation to dinner on special occasions."

"So you are saying I've been spoiled?"

"I'm saying the single women and mothers with eligible daughters had hoped for a chance. Since your attention didn't turn to them when your fiancée didn't arrive, they are not pleased."

The logic made sense, even if taking out their anger on Rose's Rescue didn't. He'd never considered any of the women or girls in the congregation as potential brides.

Reverend Green finished first. "I'll clean up here so you can go sweep out the church before it gets too warm."

The tradition of cleaning the building early Monday morning and again on Saturday evening had been established by

Reverend Green and his wife when the church was first built. Occasionally, parishioners wishing for guidance would come help as an excuse to talk.

With a pail of water in one hand and the mop and broom over his shoulder, Lewis crossed the yard to the church. As he rounded the corner, his stomach plummeted. Tacked to the church door, was Saturday's newspaper. Large handwritten black letters proclaimed:

THE REVEREND HAS NO BUSINESS WITH PROSTI-
TUTES.

He set the pail on the step and leaned the broom and mop against the banister. Few people were about, and no one seemed to watch from the buildings across the street. Hands trembling with anger, Lewis removed the tack and the newspaper, and then opened the door. The church was never locked. The few hymnals were not worth stealing, and the harmonium was too big to remove from the building with ease.

The large Bible lay open on the pulpit. Lewis rarely used it during his sermons, preferring to write out the scriptures he quoted. When he left, he stored the Bible on the shelf inside the pulpit.

A piece of paper lay in the open book.

EPHESIANS 5:5

REVEREND, NEITHER ARE YOU WELCOME HERE

Lewis glanced at the verse to be sure he remembered it correctly. He took a deep breath and looked up at the ceiling, praying for strength. He was no whoremonger. Yet someone obviously believed it true. He looked around the church again. Nothing else was out of place. Lewis folded the papers and put them in his pocket. He would show them to Reverend Green and TJ later.

For now, he would proceed as if nothing had occurred. He moved the pail, broom, and mop inside and started cleaning. Wiping down the pews gave him time to contemplate. No answers came. He could envision none of the single women or their mothers tacking the hateful note to the door. The mere fact there were no misspellings in the notes eliminated nearly half of the congregation as suspects.

By the time the chapel was clean, Lewis's anger had given way to curiosity and worry that someone might threaten the Rescue as well. Removing Lewis from the congregation would be as simple as a few letters to Austin. Thus far, Reverend Green's proposal that Lewis work as his junior had pacified the local leadership. The newspaper article could change that quickly.

On the other hand, Rose's Rescue was not so easy to relocate as a junior minister. TJ monitored Rose's since his wife founded it. For the town and Emily's safety, the sheriff needed to know the threat may be growing.

Lewis shut the chapel doors as TJ rode up. "Sheriff, I was about to come find you."

TJ dismounted and left his horse in the shade of a pecan tree. "You didn't happen to find a message written on Saturday's paper did you?"

"How did you know?" Lewis pulled the papers out of his pocket.

"Miss Clara found one tacked on the back door of the Rescue this morning. I thought I would see if you'd received one too."

"I was going to bring them over to you as soon as I finished here. Whoever wrote my messages must have some education. Not a single word is misspelled, and the lettering is almost as good as that of a sign painter. Neither Reverend Green nor I have used Ephesians 5:5 as the text for a sermon since I've been here, so they must read too."

"That leaves more than half the town as suspects. Was anything vandalized?"

"A tack in the front door is all. But we've put up a notice or two ourselves, so one more hole is hardly vandalism. They moved the Bible but didn't damage it."

"What about the harmonium?"

"I dusted it but didn't play it. It doesn't look damaged."

TJ took the newspaper and note from Lewis. "Let me know if you see anything suspicious."

"I will."

TJ rode off in the direction of the town square. For a moment, Lewis considered following him. Had Clara been frightened? What of the others? Interrupting their routine with a visit would likely heighten their anxiety. He would visit later and see Clara home.

⟫◆⟪

The women of Rose's Rescue were surprisingly nonplussed by Clara's discovery of the note.

"Isn't the first, won't be the last."

"Someone discovered her husband has been unfaithful and blames us."

"Probably one of the prohibitionists. They think everything is either the demon liquor's fault or ours."

Almost every woman commented a similar variation during the day. Peony told a story of a woman who found her husband with one of the girls at the first brothel she'd worked. The woman had three six shooters and used the bar for target practice, destroying the most valuable of the bottles. She saddled her husband with the debt and then left him.

Despite their nonchalance, worry tugged at Clara. Emily dismissed her fears telling her TJ had matters well in hand.

Clara smiled as she taught, but all the while, a lump formed in her stomach that twisted so tight she couldn't eat any of the luncheon that had been prepared. When classes concluded, she slipped out as quickly as she could, using the excuse of needing to go to the post office.

As she walked down the boardwalk, she examined every person who passed, wondering who could have written the note. Who could hate so much?

The postmaster shook his head when she asked if she'd received any mail. There would be no diversion from her thoughts there. Clara posted a letter home with hopes it would be answered.

When she stepped out of the post office, two women, whose names she couldn't remember, stopped talking and greeted her. Not likely them. Clara nodded a hello and hurried on.

Dr. Palmer's buggy turned the corner in front of her, and he slowed. "Would you like a ride?"

Mrs. Reese's house was barely three blocks away, yet the company would be nice. Dr. Palmer couldn't have written the letters. "Yes, please."

He reached down to hand her up rather than walking around. "I heard you had an eventful morning."

Clara looked at the doctor, not sure what to say. Did he refer to the letters or something else?

"TJ showed me the notes you and the reverend found."

"Lewis found a note too?"

Dr. Palmer glanced at her, then back at the road. Clara realized her mistake. "I've known Reverend Staples since before I can remember. He was my brother's best friend. I'm still trying to remember to use his title."

"I'm aware of your friendship. He is the other man who asked to court you." The doctor clearly meant his deduction as a statement, not a question.

"Do you mind that much?"

"It would be easier without the competition. However, I am a firm believer that without choices, we never know ourselves."

"That is a weighty thought."

"You have lived where it snows in the winter, so you will be able to decide if you prefer Southern winters. Young Donny, on the other hand, was surprised to learn that ice on ponds could become thick enough to stand on. He has no idea what he prefers since he was born and raised here."

"What about you? Do you know what you prefer in winter?"

"I am fond of a good snowstorm or two, and we usually get one that brings an inch, maybe two, each January. That's enough for me. If I am lucky, I can sit by my fire and read. If not, some fool will have tried to venture out and ended up breaking his leg, and then I am very glad it snows only once a year." Dr. Palmer laughed as he told his story.

"How long have you lived here?"

"I moved here in '72 after I completed medical school. So yes, I am nearly old enough to be your father."

"I wasn't asking that. I was curious if you knew if it was common for threats against Rose's or the place that was there before."

"I can't say for sure. I only went in Belle's place, or the Bull's Eye as she called it, when someone needed a doctor or because the law required it."

Clara tipped her head, trying to make sense of a law that made a man go to a brothel, and couldn't find a reason. "The law?"

"The prostitution licensing law requires that all the workers be in good health and examined every quarter. Most of the owners preferred the other doctor sign off as I only signed the license if the worker was healthy and wanted to work there—or rather, said they wanted to." Dr. Palmer stopped in the shade of the tree in front of Mrs. Reese's. "How much of Rose's story do you know?"

"Emily wrote how she died trying to warn her."

"Did she tell you that I could have saved Rose months earlier, but I missed the chance?"

Clara shook her head.

"When I examined the women, Belle or one of her bodyguards were always nearby. I always asked the women if they wanted to work there as I was required. Rose answered, 'As willing as Briseis.'"

"Briseis, as in the woman kidnapped in the Iliad?" Clara had read the work during her last semester.

"It took me months before I sorted out her meaning and realized she wasn't willing at all. It was days later she died in the little surgery in my home. I was too late." He shook his head and muttered something that sounded like, "I'm always too late."

Clara didn't ask him to repeat the words, sure they weren't for her. "I'm sure you did your best."

Dr. Palmer shook his head. "I wish I could believe that. And if I have not dismayed you enough, I will be thirty-six this fall. Which is likely much too old for you."

"My mother is ten years younger than my father. I don't think your age, or the story you shared, is enough to end our friendship after a few days."

Dr. Palmer nodded. "I am glad to hear it. I don't think I did much to alleviate your stress. May I call on you tonight at seven, providing I am not called away?"

"I would like that very much." The sincerity she felt surprised her. The doctor needed a friend, and so far he seemed like a kind man.

Dr. Palmer got out of the buggy and hurried around to help her down. His hand didn't linger in hers like Bernard's always had or Lewis's did when he brought her from the depot. Clara wasn't sure if there was any meaning to it, or if the doctor was just a busy man.

14

onny delivered Wednesday's newspaper to the Rescue just before the lunch break. As was their practice, Emily passed the paper around and they discussed the articles.

Rae grabbed the paper from Morning Glory as she read the first article. "I don't care if some Mexican general married some chica in San Antonio. I want to know if there is another letter about us."

Murmurs of agreement sounded from around the room.

Emily rapped on the table. "Ladies, this is not how we behave, however I understand your interest. If you will hand the paper to me." She smoothed out the paper and turned it over. For several moments, she was silent. "There is another letter in the same vein as Saturday's. Before we read it, I want to point out that just because someone wrote it, doesn't mean they understand or represent the majority of Hiramsville. Newspapers don't always print the truth."

"Why would the paper print it if it ain't true?" asked Rae.

"Isn't true. Newspapers, like any other business, want to make money. In big cities, newsboys yell out the most sensational things trying to sell the paper. Remember the two-headed chicken from Saturday? The article was only a few words long. But a newspaper boy could make it sound like the most exciting thing."

"Are you saying the two-headed chicken isn't true?"

"No, I'm saying it isn't important. I'm sure there are enough witnesses to say the chicken is real, but does it matter?"

"Not in my frying pan. He still has only two drumsticks." Nellie's comment drew enough laughter to lighten the mood.

"Very true. This letter doesn't change who you are or the lives you have reclaimed, nor does it change Reverend Staples into something he is not."

The mention of Lewis's name caused Clara's heart to skip a beat. There was no truth in the supposition that he was looking for a wife among the women at the Rescue. According to Lavender, none of the women were interested in him either. Although this denomination didn't practice confessions, several of the women had confided in either Lewis or Reverend Green, hoping to find some sort of absolution. While they trusted the ministers, the few who wished for marriage couldn't bring themselves to even consider a man of the cloth. Lewis knew better than most why Lavender and the others had no intention of ever entering wedlock.

REVEREND REFUSES TO RENOUNCE ROSE'S RESCUE

Not one word of condemnation crossed the pulpit Sunday although over half of the Rescue's women attended church for the first time.

Instead of taking the opportunity to do his duty, the reverend instead taught of joy. The topic was considered by some members of the congregation to be most inappropriate.

According to his contract, the young reverend must marry soon or else he will lose his job. Inter-

estingly, he spent his afternoon with the women
of Rose's Rescue instead of courting one of the
town's eligible bachelorettes. Rumors are circulating as to his motives. What could this mean for his
standing in the community? Should we demand
a replacement?

Petunia spoke from the back of the room where she nursed
Scotty. "That isn't fair. He has been nothing but kind to us.
I never saw him act the least bit other than gentlemanly to
any of us. The only one he's shown interest in is Clara. She
isn't a soiled dove like us. Not sayin' it matters to him, but
she ain't, and the newspaper person knows that."

Clara's face burned. Lavender had spoken of her suspicions that Lewis held her in esteem. She did not know the
others had noticed. Then, there was the other problem. Clara
turned to face Petunia. She wanted them to know she would
never judge them. "My past may be different, but I hope
you don't believe I think of you as different from me. I am
growing to love all of you as I do my sister."

"We know it doesn't matter to you, Miss Clara. I was talking
about the people who write letters like that. They see you
as acceptable, and we aren't." It was the longest statement
Daffodil had spoken in Clara's presence. "And we are all
happy that the reverend and the doctor want to court you.
Although, I am hoping the reverend wins."

"No, the doctor would be better."

Clara couldn't be sure who spoke, as now all the women
seemed to be speaking at once. Somehow, the focus had
shifted from the town wanting to oust the rescue to Clara's
courtship opportunities. She looked to Emily for help.

Emily shook her head, her eyes twinkling with laughter.

Clara stood. No one seemed to pay attention, so she
knocked on the table three times. The room quieted. "I had
no idea when I said I loved you all like my sisters that you

would plan my life like she would too. As for the doctor and the reverend, it isn't a competition. Neither one is going to win me like a prize at a potato sack race or a medieval duel. If I marry anyone, it will be because I believe that he cares for me and I care for him. It will be because I can laugh with him and want to stand by him. I don't want to be some trophy for my husband to bring out at parties and show his friends." Some of the women looked chagrined and even downcast. Clara didn't want to cast a cloud on their spirits. "If and when I marry, I will invite you all, and we will have the grandest celebration ever."

With everyone smiling again, Clara sat back down.

"So what should we do about the articles? Write to the newspaper ourselves?" asked Peony.

"What do you think you should do?" Emily turned the question back to them.

"You and Mrs. Reese talked about moving Rose's to the unfinished hotel on the river. It gives us more room and—" Nellie looked at a few of the others before she spoke. "Even though this place has been fixed up right nice, for those of us who worked with Belle, it brings back memories. For the ones that didn't work here… it was still a brothel."

Emily nodded. "We have discussed those points before. The problem is that even if we can sell this place at a profit, the hotel costs more. Which is probably why the investors abandoned the project when the other hotel opened two miles north at the Springs. We don't have the funds at this time, but we are working on getting closer."

"We could hold a dinner or something to raise money. If they want us to go so bad, you'd think they would pay to see us go. My ma's church held benefits all the time." Rae's suggestion had some merit; however, twenty dollars here and fifteen dollars there would hardly buy the hotel any time in this decade.

"That is a good idea, but it doesn't solve the problem of the newspaper," said Lavender. "What should we do about that?"

"Nothing. You pretend it didn't happen. Don't allow them to intimidate us. It is only words. Like Miss Emily said, it is just one person's opinion," said Daffodil.

"Sound reasoning, however I think we should also be more aware of, well, everything. Sometimes words lead to actions." Lavender shuddered.

There was knowledge behind her statement that came from those secrets that all the women had.

Nellie interrupted everyone's thoughts with a more pressing matter. "Lunchtime!"

Clara waited for the others to get their food. There was still one question no one had answered. What did this article mean for Lewis's future?

⟫◆⟪

Donny sat on the bench below Rose's Rescue's largest window.

"Is this seat taken?" Lewis pointed to the empty half of the bench.

"Nope. You can have a seat if you'd like."

"Any trouble today?"

"Just a heap of folk staring at the place. The paper has 'em all curious. Why are you here?"

"To show people that I won't be intimidated by the newspaper."

"Not because you've been late the last two evenings and missed escorting Miss Clara home?"

Lewis ran a finger around his collar. "That is another reason."

"I thought so. Doc is on a call and not likely to get here anyway."

It wouldn't be right to hope that Doc's call would take a long time, since Doc was likely with one of the parishioners. "Have you heard many people talk about Rose's lately?"

"Mostly speculating on who would have written the newspaper. A few folks are thinking the article is right, since this is the corner of the square and all." Donny sliced the stick he was carving. "Nellie thinks it is because some of those wives are worried that their husband went to Belle's and don't want reminders. Especially sittin' in the church. Hypocrites."

"Those are interesting observations."

"But I think the real reason is you ain't married. You shoulda married your fiancée's twin—them being the same and all."

No one who knew Clara and Catherine would ever think they were the same beyond looks. Catherine's lighthearted personality would never be confused with Clara's reserved thoughtfulness. Catherine took risks—to jump on ideas without a second thought of the consequences or others. Clara preferred to observe and think before acting, although she often was goaded to things before she was ready. Of course, why hadn't he seen that a year ago? Clara would never give an immediate answer to a proposal. Not then, not now. "There is a gigantic difference between looking alike and being alike."

"Ya don't say."

"Yes, and I was dimwitted enough to not understand that sooner."

"Understand what?"

Lewis shook his head. "I don't think I could explain even if I tried."

Donny shrugged. "That's what grownups always say."

"Sometimes it is true. If I'm just understanding something after twenty-years, it may be another twenty before I have the words for it."

"That is a long time." Donny folded his pocketknife and put it in his pocket. He pointed across the street to the clock tower. "And it is time for class to be over. I hope Nellie made something good today."

The boy dashed around the building to the kitchen door in the alley.

A few minutes later, Clara exited, still tying the ribbon to her hat. "Good afternoon. Is it presumptuous to think you are waiting for me?"

Lewis looked in the window. Several pairs of eyes looked back. "Did you come to that conclusion yourself or was it a consensus?"

A blush colored her cheeks. "It was a topic of interest the last few minutes. Apparently, you have been too late the last two days, and I had already left."

Lewis extended his arm. "Might I be so bold as to ask if I may escort you home?"

"Yes, I suppose that would be acceptable," Clara looked up to meet his gaze. "Though I do need to stop by the post office first. I am hoping for a letter."

"A detour I need to make as well. Have you heard from home yet?"

"No. I thought my mother would have written by now even if she had gone to the Cape."

Lewis didn't ask about Catherine. There was no way to broach the subject without bringing pain to Clara. "The last letter from my mother was written the day of your departure."

Clara took his offered arm. "I want to know what my parents think of me. If they believe the truth."

Lewis waited for a wagon before crossing the street, careful to keep them from stepping in muck.

Clara lifted her skirt as she crossed the dirt road. "It seems as if letters are the cause of many problems."

"You mean the one in the newspaper?" he asked.

"Yes. The women are worried that it could get worse. As for me, I am concerned that your reputation is being besmirched."

"I have done nothing to be ashamed of. I believe the principal complaint is my status as a bachelor." Lewis paused in front of the post office to allow a customer to leave. He held the door for Clara.

"Miss Taylor, I have two letters for you." The postmaster pulled the letters from a slot and checked the address. "Oh, this one is addressed to Catherine Taylor or Staples. I'm afraid I can't give it to you."

"Please, is there a return direction? My sister played an elaborate joke on some people. It may be for me."

The postmaster squinted then pulled a pair of glasses from off the top of his head. "Ah, it says Clara and New York. Very smudged."

"I could hardly write to myself. It must be my sister."

"I should only give the letter to the addressee."

Lewis tapped Clara's shoulder and nodded for her to move aside. "If I may, Catherine often tried to trade places with Clara. I do believe it is a joke between sisters."

"Well, since both names are on the envelope, and you are the only Taylor in town … Come to think of it, it looks much like the handwriting on the ones the reverend used to receive." The postmaster handed over the letter with a thicker envelope. "And Reverend, I have one for you as well."

Lewis waited until they were well away to speak. "Do you think it is from Catherine?"

"It must be. The other is from my parents and addressed to me. I've waited days for this correspondence, and now I dread opening either letter."

"Would you like me to stay nearby while you read them? If you wish to talk …"

Clara bit her lip.

"And if you don't wish to talk, I will not press you. I won't even watch you read. I have my own missive."

"Is there a place along the river to sit? I'd rather not have Becky or Mrs. Reese know I have the letters."

"There are a few fallen logs. Nothing grand." Lewis would be sure to check that they were clear of any snakes.

"That will do."

Lewis led her a block west to the river and to the path along its banks. A promising log sat under the shade of a live oak a few feet from the river. "Let me check for any critters before you sit."

"Critters?"

"You know, unwanted animals."

Clara shivered as she dropped his arm. "Not Boston Common is it?"

"No." Lewis circled the log and gave it a kick. He then pulled out the bandana a woman in the congregation had given him some time ago. The larger cloth was more useful in the West than the handkerchief he'd carried in Boston. "However, it is much quieter than walking along the Charles River—and no train tracks."

Clara sat carefully and opened her parents' letter. The sound of the river amplified in the silence.

Lewis broke the seal on his mother's letter. As he suspected, his mother's letter was full of shock and a need for smelling salts. It appeared as if she wrote it over several days as her thoughts became more coherent. It ended with a demand that Lewis wed Clara to "save everyone's reputations." Mother had been talking to Mrs. Taylor and thought it was the only way to fix things.

Clara sighed and folded her pages together. She watched the river for several minutes.

Lewis tucked the pages of his mother's letter into his pocket.

Clara sighed again. "If I married you, how much of your problems would end?"

"As you pointed out last week, marrying me to end my problems isn't a good reason to marry."

"That was before the letters to the editor. And everything." She waved a hand to encompass the entirety of Texas. An exaggeration of their current situation; Massachusetts was more the size of their problems, or maybe Rhode Island.

Lewis turned, pulling his knee up on the log so he could see Clara better. "'And everything'? Did your family write something to make you think you should marry me?"

Clara looked at her hands. "They cannot confirm where Catherine is. Father is going to New York. Rumors are circulating. Father is of the opinion I should come home while there is still a chance to make a match for me. Mother writes that I should fulfill my duty to you."

"Duty? How is marrying me your duty?"

"I am Catherine's twin. I always clean up the messes. Although I rarely get credit for it."

Lewis reached for Clara's hand. Only last week he would have accepted her proposal to save his job. She would never be happy if he did now. Yes, she would stay by his side and fulfill her role as the preacher's wife and in time bear him children. All because of duty. "This is the same logic I used on you not ten days ago. If it was wrong then, it is wrong now. No Clara, you can't marry me out of duty."

Her hat bounced as her head jerked up. Her eyes met his. "But I thought that is what you wanted. To make me your wife and keep your post."

"Those are the wrong reasons to marry you. You told me so yourself. Why would that change?"

⋘◆⋙

Inconceivable. He had begged her to marry him, and now Lewis was turning down her offer. Clara looked down at his hand holding hers. Lovers held hands. Engaged couples held hands. Men who were refusing to accept an acceptance to their previously denied proposal did not hold hands.

"Clara, why?" His blue eyes filled with sadness as he rubbed the back of her hand, sending a zap of longing through her. Even if he didn't love her as she loved him, she knew they could have a better marriage than one her father planned for her.

"Because I don't wish to return to Boston to be thrown into a loveless marriage by my father."

"Why can't you stay here? Do your job?"

"Because they would be disappointed in me. Mother didn't want me to come, but she figured that with Catherine here..."

"Didn't they realize you were the responsible one? That Catherine usually started the trouble?"

"How do you know that?"

"I lived next door to you my entire life. How could I not know—from the very first time Catherine convinced you to climb the tree." Lewis smiled at the memory.

"You helped me down."

"Well, the cat got himself down. I wouldn't have been much of a gentleman if I left you up there."

"You were only ten. Did you know Catherine chased him up that tree? She told me to climb on her back so I could reach the first branch then we could get him down. Then she left me." No one ever believed that part of the story.

"I saw it all from my bedroom window. When she ran inside, I thought she was going for help."

"Why didn't you tell my parents she tricked me into climbing the tree?"

"I did when I brought you home." Lewis touched her cheek with a single finger, then dropped his hand. "Catherine had already told her tale."

"See, you do know me. We could be happy."

Lewis pulled his hand away and scooted back on the log, breaking all physical connection. "I knew you then.

But I don't know you now. We both deserve better than forcing ourselves into a marriage—to save my job, quiet a letter writer, or please our families. Thirty years from now, I don't want either one of us to wonder why we got married."

"I told you I liked you." More than liked, but other than a few conversations over the last few years, there had been little contact.

Lewis picked at the bark of the tree. "Last year, if I had proposed to the right sister, what would you have said?"

She'd asked herself the same question many times. Likely she would have accepted, although not as fast as Catherine. "I don't know."

"Yes, you do. You would have told me you needed to think about it. You might have even asked me why I never courted you. Given long enough, you may have told me no because you would have reached the conclusion I was asking because I'd been jilted and I needed a wife quickly. You were my best chance."

"You were jilted?" That piece of gossip had never reached her or Catherine. Although Lewis was a favorite at society balls, he'd never danced even twice with the same person. Well, not since her first ball.

"Didn't your brother tell you?"

"Tell me what?" She was never Clifford's confidant. Catherine was the one who knew his secrets.

"How he met Pricilla."

"He said you introduced them. I don't think he was ever clear on where or how. But we were in our first year at Bradford, and you know my brother doesn't write."

Lewis looked at the river. "I had taken her to the symphony. I can't blame Clifford. She liked him better, and it was the better match."

"Is that why you missed his wedding?" She had expected Lewis to stand up with Clifford.

"Not exactly. I asked him to have it the weekend I had my last exams so I couldn't come. It was best for both of us. We had a terrible argument over that and some other things."

Clara ignored the curious "other things," and kept on topic. "Then you proposed three weeks after his wedding? Do you still love her?"

"I don't think I ever did. I was more angry at Clifford than anything."

"So you proposed to Catherine, me, us to get back at him?"

Lewis sighed. "No. I had wanted to court you since your first ball, but your brother and I had come to an agreement that I wouldn't."

"My first ball? When I was sixteen? That was years ago. Why didn't you say something?"

"I promised your brother I wouldn't…"

Clara had waited days for him to call after he'd danced not once, but twice with her, saving her from being a wallflower at her first ball. "The black eye? You had a black eye the next day in church, and Clifford had a bruise on his cheek."

"He was adamant that I not court his sisters. We'd agreed years earlier that neither of us would date the others sister or sisters. That night, he hadn't approved of the second dance. A first dance was tolerable, as our parents would expect it. But then I couldn't leave you standing alone during your first waltz. Not after Catherine had managed to convince every man who tried to approach you to dance with her instead."

"You were watching?"

"After sixteen years it was a habit to watch out for you."

"So you didn't court me because of a fight?"

"No, because of the agreement. When we were seven or eight, we cut our hands and became blood brothers. It was very popular among the boys at school. Then we decided we could never marry each other's sisters because we were brothers." Lewis barked out a laugh. "It seemed logical then. Clifford took the oath seriously."

"So after that ball, you never thought of courting me?"

"I thought about it, but my friendship came first. Until Clifford put it last."

The shadows from the tree stretched almost all the way across the river. They'd been here much longer than she'd anticipated. "I should get to Mrs. Reese's. They are likely wondering where I am."

Lewis stood and offered his arm. "Are you still willing to go to the violinist on Friday night?"

"Yes. Why wouldn't I?"

"Because I believe I just refused your offer of marriage."

Clara tapped her letters on her skirt. "Thank you for keeping me from doing something rash."

After supper, Clara retired to her room to reread Catherine's letter. She'd been too nervous to more than skim over it with Lewis there, and it hadn't made sense.

C—

We are having a wonderful week at Niagara Falls. B. has been so attentive. We have had one problem after another with the wedding. First, we were too late to see the justice of the peace. Then he was at lunch. B. reassures me that unlike Massachusetts, New York honors common-law marriages. He is annoyed because he feels I am too thick about the middle. I told him it is only because he sees me without a corset on. I cannot wait to meet his family.

I'm sure you understand how little time I have to write. Is marriage and being with him as lovely as I told you?

Love,

C.

At least Catherine was alive. The letter lacked the details Clara had expected. Nothing about the hotel, or the people. Not even her dress. Clara folded the letter away. She knelt by her bed, and prayed for her sister, the women at the Rescue, and for Lewis. The last part she left rather vague as it was hard to know what to ask when they'd both agreed marrying for his job was not the correct step. The peace that followed prayer filled her. Things would work out, eventually.

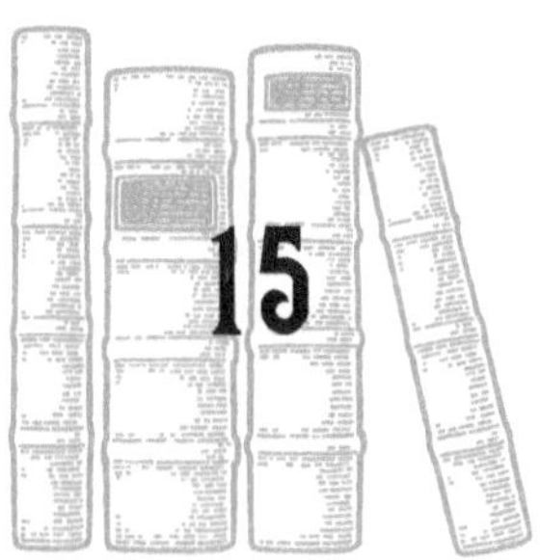

riday morning, Reverend Green found a note wedged between the spindles of his rocking chair on the porch of the manse. The only day they had not received a threatening note at the church, or the house so far had been Wednesday. Of course, that had been the newspaper day, so no personal note had been necessary. The entire town read the letter.

Reverend Green handed the note to Lewis. "I wasn't sure, when you suggested that I give the sermon this week; however, I believe you are right. A week or two of me seeming to take the reins might calm things down."

"Have you heard anything from Austin?"

"Just a letter agreeing to my proposition of keeping you here and the two of us working together. Which is good. I don't think they will make a surprise visit. You have done nothing I wouldn't have done."

"Tonight I'm taking Clara to the violinist. Perhaps being seen publicly courting her will help."

"She teaches at the school, and like Miss Emily, she is a Northerner. As are you. Neither fact is in your favor."

Reverend Green used one foot to set his rocker in motion.

"You're from Boston too." Their sect's only seminary was in Massachusetts. All of the ministers were schooled there.

"Yes, but I've been in Texas since '37. Texas was its own country then. Most people don't think of me as anything other than Texan."

Lewis refolded the note. "I better take this to TJ. He will want to know about it, even if he can't do anything other than collect the notes."

Everyone he met on the way to the Sheriff's office either smiled or nodded. Lewis removed them from his mental suspect list.

TJ sat in his office, surrounded by crates full of books and other household items.

"Did someone steal a library, Sheriff?"

"No," TJ replied, shaking his head. "We are moving tomorrow. I had no idea my wife had this many books in the house. I can't figure out where she kept them all. I'd seen her buy a book or two, but there must be three hundred here."

The move—wasn't that next week? Lewis hadn't announced it at church or requested help. He needed to love his neighbor more and worry about himself less. "Maybe you should start a library."

"The new house is big enough. I still can't decide if I'll miss this place or not. I've spent most of my adult life living below the jail. At least I won't have prisoners sleeping right above my baby's head."

Lewis sat in the chair across the desk from his friend. "I thought the new house was a week or more from being done."

"When my brother was here, he helped a bit. My new deputy is tired of living at the hotel, so he has been working on the house too. GW is passing through on the way back to Waco tomorrow with a couple of his friends. I figured

I'd give the rangers a day of hard labor for all the meals we've cooked for them over the years. According to Emily, the place still needs some paint and paper, but she can work around the boxes."

"I can lend a hand too."

"Appreciate that. What brought you here? I'm sure it wasn't to volunteer to heft books across town."

"Another note." Lewis dropped the paper in the center of TJ's desk.

TJ sighed as he picked it up. "The Rescue got a warning too. Only someone painted it on the backside of the building before sunrise this morning."

"I didn't notice a message when I walked past Rose's."

"Paint was still wet when Donny found it. After he showed me, I gave him the job of washing it off. There was some paint left over from when they painted the place last fall. He probably finished covering it up." TJ unfolded the note.

"Did Donny see the culprit?"

"Just the people he normally does. The butcher and the baker got an early start on the day. Livery was open. Collins was in the print shop. He keeps all sorts of odd hours. I questioned him. Collins insists he didn't write the letter but won't show me or tell me more. Freedom of the press and all."

"Did anyone see anything unusual?" Lewis couldn't think of a single suspect.

"No. Likely that is why they painted on the back of the building. Too much of a chance of getting caught if they were to paint on the front." TJ refolded the note, opened a drawer, and added it to others. "I've assigned either the deputies or myself to walk around the square and down to the church in the middle of the night. We've missed them every time."

"You keep saying 'them.' You think it is more than one person?"

"The painting was done with two different brushes, and the first of both sentences was drier than the last—likely two painters. The notes look like two or three handwriting styles. Emily thinks it could be one person trying to write in different ways. I'm not so sure."

"Is there anything to be done?"

The sheriff shook his head. "Emily and Mrs. Reese wrote another letter of inquiry to the investor that started to build the abandoned hotel. They hope that since it has been six months since they last inquired, he will lower his price."

"I didn't think they would be scared into moving." The women at the Rescue where tougher than old horseshoe nails to choose to make a new life. They wouldn't abandon their goals easily.

"Emily agrees with you. One of the problems with the current location is that the building was a brothel. Even the women who didn't work or live there feel the ghosts— I don't have a better word—haunting them from the past. The current building would make a good restaurant. Mrs. Reese thinks a boarding house and restaurant would work—if they can sell it to a buyer who doesn't want to return it to its former use."

"What about safety? There is so little out by the abandoned hotel project." Men occasionally walked into Rose's demanding services. Someone was always nearby if things got out of hand.

"I'll cross that bridge when I come to it."

Lewis left the Sheriff's office with more questions than when he started. He walked the long way around the square, stopping to talk to everyone on the way. He hoped for some clue pointing to the elusive note writer. As he passed Rose's, he looked through the window. The usual flurry of activity preceding market day swirled through the room in a blur of speed. Fingers flew over sewing machines, pinning, snipping, and stitching. Other women worked at two pressing boards ironing clothes, while another woman carried large baskets of folded clothes out of the backroom. Clara was nowhere in sight. Experience told him his help wasn't necessary or wanted. Miss Petunia looked up. He waved and walked on.

⸺⬦⸺

The silver handled hairbrush clattered as it hit the wood floor. Clara groaned as she bent to pick it up. No matter how she tried to arrange her hair, she wasn't satisfied. Catherine was so much better at the latest styles.

Nellie tapped on the open door. "Would you like some help?"

"Please. I am all thumbs for fingers. I'm afraid Lewis will be ashamed to be seen with me."

"I doubt that." Nellie eased the pins out of Clara's hair. "Petunia is sure he was looking for you this morning."

"He has to pass by Rose's one way or another to get to the Sheriff's office."

"Petunia says his ears turned pink when she waved. He was embarrassed to be caught." Nellie brushed and twisted Clara's hair into a style from the latest magazine.

"How do you do that? I've been trying for the past hour to do something other than my usual bun."

"I started working on my mother's hair when I was young. Belle had me assist the workers who were too far gone on drink or opium to do their own hair before she would allow them downstairs."

"In Boston, there are shops where women can have their hair styled. You could run one of those shops."

"Like a barber shop for women?"

"Yes. Only they don't always cut hair, sometimes they just pin it up and curl it."

"And people go to such a place?" Nellie wove a ribbon through Clara's hair.

"Yes. I suppose you would need a larger city to make a go of it. So there would be enough women who wanted help with their hair yet can't afford a maid."

Nellie shook her head. "I'm not moving to any of the big cities. No one is going to allow someone who looks like me to fix their hair."

Clara looked at Nellie's reflection in the mirror. "Maybe once they get to know you…"

"Most people just don't take that much time." Nellie added another hair pin and stood back. "There you go."

Clara turned sideways to see the full effect of the intricate hair style. "Oh Nellie. It is gorgeous."

"Do you need help with your dress?"

"No, thank you."

Clara closed the door behind Nellie and turned to her dress lying on the bed. The fluttery feeling in her stomach increased rather than dissipating with the difficulty of over-coming her hair.

"It is only Lewis." Whispering the words out loud didn't help. Nevertheless, she repeated the mantra a dozen times while changing her skirt and bodice. She contemplated taking a bit of bicarbonate, but didn't want her breath to smell of it. Instead she ate a peppermint, which solved the problem until Lewis knocked on the front door. Her stomach did flip flops the moment he smiled at her.

The walk to the theater did little to calm her nerves. Speaking with Dr. Palmer never left her in such a state, but then again, Dr. Palmer never spoke of marriage either. The wife of a doctor would not be expected to take on as many responsibilities as the wife of a preacher, although both would be expected to be pillars of the community. If she'd stayed in Boston, Father would have encouraged a match where she would have been expected to be seen among the town's elite. The chances of her marrying a farmer or a shopkeeper and living in anonymity were close to none no matter where she lived.

Fortunately for her swirling mind and stomach, Lewis spoke of generalities, avoiding anything to do with their families, which was preferable, especially since she would have no answer if he asked about Catherine's cryptic letter. He also avoided talking of Rose's, although they both waved at Scotty as they walked in front of the building to the theater next door.

Hiramsville's theater and opera house was neither opulent nor shabby. The slope of the seating area allowed for all to see the stage, unless one was unfortunate enough to sit behind a pillar. It wasn't large enough to have box seats, despite the large stage that could accommodate the size of most productions.

Lewis escorted her to their row. Several people were forced to stand so they could reach their seats. They greeted the people around them. Lewis seemed to know everyone, including those not of his congregation.

A moment later, the gas lights dimmed, and the violinist took the stage. Like the building, the performance was enjoyable, being neither exquisite or poor. An ensemble played with the violinist, adding texture to the performance. Clara waved her fan to clear her thoughts. Somehow, upon entering the theater, her internal critique had come in her mother's voice and style. Clara pushed it out of her mind. Mother was far too critical of everything.

During the next piece, she was surprised by the feather-light touch of Lewis's hand on hers. It at once calmed her thoughts and caused the flutters in her stomach to increase ten-fold. His fingers explored the back of her hand and then her palm. All thoughts of the violinist's skills fled, and the remainder of the concert blurred together as Lewis drew his thumb across her skin.

As the gas lights brightened, Lewis withdrew his hand and smiled at her before clapping with the rest of the audience.

Dr. Palmer stood with a woman she didn't recognize three rows in front of her. It didn't bother her at all to see him with someone else. So much for her experiment. Courting Dr. Palmer had done nothing to heal her childhood crush on Lewis. Horse feathers!

Lewis put his hand on her elbow to guide her out of the row. This time, Clara allowed herself to acknowledge the effect of his touch. A year of trying to be interested in other men, anger over his proposal to her sister, and trying not to follow everyone's expectations had not altered the infatuation that had been her constant companion for nearly a decade. If anything, her attraction had grown deeper.

They reached the end of the row. Lewis removed his hand and offered Clara his arm. It was not his touch that sent a thrill through her this time, but rather the soft smile he gave her. Double horse feathers and dull hat pins. She had fallen worse than a heroine in a Gothic novel. If she told Lewis of her feelings after Wednesday's conversation, he would find her as changeable as an April day in Boston—sunny one moment and raining the next with unexpected winds.

Several people paused their exit to say good night to Reverend Lewis, and by extension to Clara. No one required any substantial conversation, allowing Clara to nod and say good night without putting any thought into the action.

The sun had set while they were in the theater, and stars dotted the sky. The temperature had dropped from sweltering to overly warm—or what locals called "much cooler."

"Would you care for a walk around the square before we return?" asked Lewis.

"Lead the way."

"It is a shame there is no place to sit and have an ice or something."

Not wishing for the evening to end, Clara grew bold. "There is some leftover ice cream in Mrs. Reese's ice room in the cellar. I doubt she would be opposed to us finishing it off."

"Leftover ice cream. I was unaware that such a thing existed. Should we shorten our walk?"

"No." Clara didn't tell him that Thelma's new recipe had proven too tart to be enjoyed. "As much as you like ice cream, I relish walking in relative coolness when all the bugs are asleep."

Lewis smiled and turned to take the long way home.

⇒◆⇐

After Wednesday's conversation, Lewis expected Clara to do no more than fulfill her obligation to attend the concert with him. Suggesting a post-concert treat and allowing extra time for the walk was a surprise. As was allowing him to hold her hand through most of the performance. Touching her had not been his plan. He'd merely wished to draw her attention to Miss Lavender and Miss Peony who sat two rows behind them. When Clara hadn't moved her hand, he'd wondered how long she would allow his caress. To his delight, she never drew her hand away and even returned his attention. Why? She'd left him with little hope only two days ago.

Lewis desperately needed answers to his questions. He started with the dullest of openings. "What did you think of the violinist?"

"She was better than I expected." Clara covered her mouth with her free hand. "I sound very much like my mother, don't I? I'm afraid I saw the building and the concert through her eyes. I had no idea that I could be so judgmental."

"I admit, I had the same reaction to many things when I came here. We are used to ornate halls and crystal chandeliers. It is hard not to compare."

"Both of our mothers would be shocked at Hiramsville Society, I think."

Lewis led her down the steps to the street, checking for anything that might soil her shoes or skirt. "As would our fathers. Can you imagine my father stepping onto the dirt street?"

"Mine would demand to know where the pavers are." Clara lifted her skirt higher as they ascended the steps onto the boardwalk on the other side of the street.

"There is a plan to brick the roads around the square. But I doubt it will happen for years yet." Other couples had the same idea as Lewis and wandered about the square.

TJ walked toward them with his brother and what must be another ranger.

"Good evening, Sheriff." Clara greeted them first.

TJ touched the brim of his hat. "Reverend, Miss Clara. I believe you have both met my brother, GW."

"You were at the depot when I arrived?" Clara tipped her head back to look at the tall man.

"Yes, ma'am." GW pointed over his shoulder. "And this is Jax. He tends to follow me around."

"Don't listen to him, ma'am. I tend to go where trouble is, and *he* is always in my way." The man's mustache didn't cover the humor in his face.

"I hope there is no trouble here. Well, at least not to warrant the Texas Rangers' involvement." Clara glanced across the square to Rose's, then she looked at Lewis with questions in her eyes.

"Fellas, Miss Clara works with my wife at Rose's. She found a couple of the notes." GW and Jax nodded at TJ's explanation.

Jax's jaw clenched tight, and his eyes narrowed as he looked across the square. "It's a shame that someone can't understand the good that Rose's does. I wish there were more places like it."

"We will let the two of you continue your walk," said GW.

"Reverend, did you lock up the church?" asked Jax.

"Couldn't, even if I wanted to. There is no lock on the door."

"Mind if I bunk down on one of the pews?" asked Jax. "I want to keep watch on the backside of Rose's and the church is closer."

"You could stay at the manse where it is more comfortable."

"I'm used to sleeping on the ground, Reverend. Besides, your place doesn't have a view of the road."

Lewis raised a brow. The ranger wasn't planning on sleep. "You are welcome to stay. We consider the church a refuge for all."

"Thank you." Jax nodded and the three men continued on.

Lewis and Clara moved on to the third side of the square. Fewer people walked there.

"Is that usual for the Rangers to take such interest in a handful of notes?"

Lewis pondered what he could say without betraying confidence. "It is rare for Jax to come to town without another woman entering the Rescue."

"You mean he brings them here?"

"It could be a coincidence."

Clara stopped and turned to see his full face. "Or this is a confidential matter you can't tell me?"

"I am afraid I have some of those. It comes with the job. I'll always have secrets to keep, even from my wife." There, he had managed to turn the conversation to a more personal subject.

"How much could you tell your wife?"

"Inevitably, she would be privy to some matters. Reverend Green was careful to counsel women with his wife either visible out of earshot or with her outside of the door. Occasionally, the women invited his wife in. He said it sent a clear message about boundaries. Sadly, some ministers have given into temptations."

"Do you counsel women often?"

"When I can, I refer them to Reverend Green. At Rose's, I try to have someone else in attendance or just outside the door. When I first arrived, several of the women in the area had questions of doctrinal import that they forgot the moment I asked them to see Reverend Green." Lewis reached down and took her free hand in his. "My wife would have to avoid the temptation to gossip."

Clara met his gaze. "I don't consider myself to be one to carry and tell tales."

Was she trying to tell him she would make a good preacher's wife? "I didn't think you were."

Lewis dropped her hand and resumed walking. "I would always tell my wife where I was. Likely, she would be the first to know of the births and passings in town."

"Or the last. One of our teachers, a widowed missionary, told us her husband would forget that some things were not confidential and forget to tell her."

"I suppose that could happen." Lewis slowed his step as he reached Mrs. Reese's street. "Although, I would hope my wife would correct me if I did."

"You believe there is room in a marriage for wives and husbands to counsel together?"

"Definitely." Lewis watched her reaction.

Clara nodded slightly but didn't turn to him. She waited a moment before speaking. "Do you still want ice cream?"

"Yes."

"I should warn you there is a reason it is left over. Thelma experimented…"

"You know I'm not staying for the ice cream, right?"

The light of the full moon illuminated Clara's blush. Perhaps he had a chance to earn her heart.

"I'll go get the key and a lantern."

Clara returned a few moments later without her hat and carrying a lit lantern. She handed Lewis the lantern.

The cool air of the cellar swirled around them. Lewis speculated the real reason for the lock may have been to keep the cool air in.

Clara spread her arms out wide. "I think I would live down here if I could. At least in the summer."

"I felt that way last summer when I was in Austin." Lewis set the lantern down on the barrel outside of the door to the ice room.

Clara slipped into the room before him. She brushed aside sawdust that surrounded a frost-covered canning jar wedged between two ice blocks. Clara picked it up with her ungloved hands. "Oh, that's cold."

Lewis grabbed a cloth from a peg to cover his hands and took the jar from Clara. "Did you freeze your hands?"

"No, I was just surprised. I should know better." She exited the room and closed the door behind him. From her sleeve, she produced a spoon. "Set it down on the barrel and try it. It will save us a trip back down here if you don't like it."

"It is ice cream, it can't be that bad." He opened the lid and scooped out a generous spoonful. "Do you have a spoon?"

Clara shook her head. "I've already tried it."

Cold creaminess bathed Lewis's tongue. He didn't understand her objection. As he swallowed, the tartness hit, causing him to close his eyes and wince. It took a moment for the feeling to pass.

Clara covered her mouth as she laughed.

Lewis returned the lid to the jar. "What is in that?"

"I'm not sure. Thelma hoped it would get milder with time. Your face says otherwise." Clara ducked her head.

"You have a bit of sawdust—" Lewis lifted it from the curl in front of her ear. His palm brushed her cheek. Clara froze. Her eyes flitted to his, then down.

Lewis dropped his hand. "I would like to kiss you, but I don't want to make the same mistake I made last time."

She lifted her chin and searched his eyes. Remarkably, she leaned forward.

"Rose's Rescue is on fire!"

The shout pulled them apart.

16

lara ran out of the cellar, Lewis on her heels.

"The Rescue is on fire!" Another shout came from the front of the house.

Lewis thrust the key and the lantern into Clara's hands. "I need to–"

"Go. Be safe."

Thelma emerged from the back door. "Do you have the key?"

Clara nodded.

"Get the extra buckets and some blankets. I'll get the laundry wagon."

Mrs. Reese came out wearing her wrapper. "Good, Clara, you are still dressed. Bring as many of the girls as you can back here. We'll make room."

Clara froze between the two conflicting orders.

Mrs. Reese held out her hands for the lantern and the key. "I'll get the things. Becky is getting dressed. Hurry! Nellie stayed at the Rescue tonight."

Lifting her skirt higher than propriety allowed, Clara ran. Smoke filled the air as flames licked the second story windows. Clara's footsteps slowed. A few men stood about doing nothing. Didn't they have buckets? Where were the women? Lewis?

A clanging sound filled the air. Horses raced from the direction of the livery, pulling a wagon behind them. The hand pump fire engine arrived. The waiting men sprang into action. Clara searched again for the women. A baby cried. Scotty.

Clara turned until she found a group standing in front of the courthouse. Nellie, Petunia and Scotty, Rae, and others stood in nightdresses or wrapped in blankets.

Clara ran to them, counting each woman in her head. "Lavender? Where is Lavender?"

Wordlessly, Rae pointed to the building.

Tears made tracks down smoke-blackened faces. Eyes riveted on the growing fire, the women were transfixed as they watched the building burn with Lavender inside. No one was leaving. Clara would have to do her best to make them comfortable here. Rae's thin nightclothes stuck to her sweat-dampened skin. Clara removed her bustle overskirt and dropped it like a cape around Rae's shoulders.

Emily appeared with her arms full of blankets. Hannah carried a basket of sheets.

"Where is Peony?" asked Emily.

Clara looked around. How had she missed her?

"Look!" Nellie pointed to the front door.

TJ and Lewis carried a blanket-wrapped body out. They rushed across the street and set the blanket down and unwrapped it to reveal Peony with most of her hair gone.

"Is she...?" Clara wasn't sure if the words came from her or someone else as Dr. Palmer knelt beside the blanket.

Peony rolled over and coughed. A collective sigh escaped from the huddled women.

"Hannah, I need cool water and sheets." Dr. Palmer barked

the request without turning. Hannah thrust her remaining sheet into Clara's arms and turned to her hotel.

"Rip that sheet into pieces."

Clara and Rae shredded the sheet as fast as they could. Hannah returned with a bucket of water in one hand and a stack of sheets balanced on her head with the other.

"Dampen those." Dr. Palmer grabbed one of the sheet strips and dunked it in the water, displacing a chunk of ice. He wrapped the strip around Peony's head.

Someone shouted from the side of the building, "We need blankets!"

Emily took three steps before the doctor stopped her. "No, you sit down. I don't need an extra patient tonight."

Clara took the blankets and ran to the cross-street side of the building. A man waved her into the alley behind Rose's. Lavender's singed wrapper barely covered her torso as she shimmied down a makeshift sheet rope. The Ranger Clara had met earlier leaned out the window above her, shouting encouraging words as flames crept up the wall. Water tossed from buckets did little to slow the fire's progress. Heat radiated off the building. Instinctively, Clara took a step away only to force herself nearer again.

A flame ignited the bottom of the sheet rope. Someone threw a bucketful of water on it. TJ caught Lavender around the waist and pulled her away from the building, setting her down a few feet away. At once Clara understood the reason for Lavender's slow progress. Hot red burns covered Lavender's arms and legs. Clara laid a blanket over Lavender's back to cover what the wrapper could not.

"Don't. Let. It. Touch. Burns." Lavender coughed between each word. It wasn't possible to protect Lavender's modesty and not touch her arms or legs.

Clara held up the blanket to shield Lavender from view. "Come. Let's get you to the doctor."

Lavender took one step and moaned.

"Are your feet burned? Can you walk?"

Lavender doubled over and coughed again.

"I need help here!" Clara shouted to anyone.

GW rushed over.

"Carry her to the doctor…"

The Ranger scooped Lavender into his arms and was off before Clara finished her sentence.

A shout from above drew her attention. Consumed in flames, the sheet rope fell to the ground. Jax hung by one arm from the windowsill, flames shooting from the second story window. Below him, men threw buckets of water on the fire burning the wall and beat back flames with wet sacks.

"Hey!" Clara held the remaining blanket up, not sure if it would have any use.

No one paid attention as they fought to give the Ranger a safe place to go.

A moment later, Jax screamed as he let go of the sill and kicked off the wall with his feet. Clara covered her mouth to stifle her scream as she watched him arc away from the building, far enough to avoid the flames. Jax landed with a thud. Someone grabbed the blanket out of Clara's arms and ran to Jax.

"Get the doctor!"

Hiking up her skirts, Clara darted around the men with their buckets to find Dr. Palmer. Donny beat her there. Clara hadn't noticed the boy in the excitement.

"I need a wagon. Also a block of ice, for more cool water, delivered to my office." The doctor pulled out a key ring and handed it to Emily. He took three steps before turning and shouting to Emily. "Stay at my office."

"What can I do?" Clara asked anyone.

From where she knelt near Peony's head, Hannah pointed to Lavender. "Keep cooling the burns."

Time lost meaning as Clara dampened cloths and applied them to Lavender's red skin. Around her, people came and went. Becky made several trips with the hand wagon, bringing water and ice. The women who'd escaped Rose's found clothing ranging from men's shirts to a dress that must have been thirty years old. Only Petunia left with Scotty at Becky's insistence.

Lewis stopped by to switch out a cloth wrapped around his left hand. He'd removed his coat and rolled up his shirt sleeves since he'd rescued Peony.

"Reverend." Hannah waved him over. "Doc told you to keep that hand in water. Let me see it."

Clara glanced over her shoulder to see Lewis's injury but couldn't see anything.

"Ouch. It's starting to blister. Put your hand in that bucket and don't take it out." Hannah forced his hand into the pail.

TJ came across the lawn. "Dr. Palmer wants to bring the injured to his office."

With the help of the other men, TJ moved Lavender and Peony to the back of the wagon. "You too, Reverend. He said anyone with a blister, he wanted to see. What about the rest of you? Have you been hiding any injuries?"

Clara, Hannah, and the other women shook their heads.

Across the street, men kept fighting the fire. They focused on the wall shared with the theater, which, unlike Rose's, was built of stone. Keeping the fire from spreading to the theater roof and the buildings beyond was the best they could do.

Dense smoke billowed into the predawn sky as the flames continued to lick at the building. The front wall fell into itself, bringing the roof down with it. Firelight illuminated the grand staircase still standing in the center.

Clara stood in stunned silence with the women from the Rescue. Becky clutched her left arm, Rae her right.

The German books. Somewhere in the mass of flame and rubble were Clara's books. Clara checked her selfish thoughts. She'd only lost a few books. Those around her had lost everything. The books could be easily replaced. Behind her, a woman sobbed. Clara didn't know how to comfort so many—or even one. She tightened her grip on Rae, whose tears flowed freely.

The courthouse clock marked the hours. Mrs. Reese and Thelma joined them.

The sun climbed in the sky, illuminating the smoldering devastation. Mrs. Reese and Thelma convinced some of the other women to leave the scene.

"Arson." The whispered word repeated over and over as the women tried to understand.

The threats in the letters had come true. How could someone hate them so much?

A few feet away, Nellie spoke with a man Clara hadn't met but had seen with GW earlier. "I didn't even use the stove today—I mean, yesterday—on account of it being so warm. I made the food in Mrs. Reese's summer kitchen and brought it over. I tell you smoke was rising from the floor. The fire started in the caves."

"The caves?" asked the man.

Nellie put her hands on her hips. "Ask the other Rangers. They were in them last year."

"I see. So you had no reason to start a fire deliberately."

"I had all the reasons in the world. I was born and raised in that building. No one hates it more than I do. But Miss Emily turned the Bull's Eye into a place to be proud of. You should be asking questions of the *good townspeople* who've been sending all the threatening letters. Not the women who lived here. 'Sides, if one of us was going to burn the place down, we'd be smart enough to do it when we were all dressed proper-like and not in the building." As Nellie's anger grew, her words became less refined.

The man moved to question Philip Tarr.

Nellie joined Becky. "Insufferable man. I thought Rangers had more brains in their head than that. He ain't worth the dime store novel version of him."

Clara tried to keep the giggle from coming up, but it escaped anyway. Rae and Becky joined in. Exhaustion fueled their response to Nellie's statement.

⟶◆⟵

With his hand submerged in cool water, Lewis grew tired of sitting. "There has to be something useful I can do."

"Pray for a miracle or two." Dr. Palmer didn't look up from where he worked on Jax.

In another room, his nurse, Emily, and Donny's mother treated the women's burns.

Heavy footfalls sounded in the hallway. TJ stuck his head in the door. "The fire is out. No one else is burned badly. A couple of men have singed hair and look like they got sunburns."

Dr. Palmer studied TJ's red face. "As do you. Have Emily put some cream on your face."

"Sure thing. How can I help?"

"I need you to hold Jax's shoulder." Dr. Palmer pointed to the spot where TJ should stand. Together, they manipulated the injured Ranger's shoulder back into place. The slightest moan escaped Jax's lips.

"I gave him enough laudanum to keep him sleepy. He didn't need to feel me reset his leg."

TJ pointed to the basin where Jax's burned hand soaked. "Can he recover from that?"

The single glimpse of the Ranger's hand when they transported him in looked much worse than the two blisters on Lewis's own.

"I don't know." Emotion choked Dr. Palmer's voice. "I'll give it some time before I..."

179

TJ shook his head and walked around the table Jax was on to the door. "I came to see if I could steal my wife away. I don't want her to exhaust herself."

"You and I both. Are you still moving today?"

TJ ran a hand down his face. "It will have to wait till next week. Most people were up helping with the fire all night. I need men to watch so we can be sure the fire is out."

"Do you know what caused it?"

"Arson."

The word sent a chill down Lewis's back. He'd hoped it had been an accident. Yet, it couldn't be a coincidence that after a week of threats, the Rescue was burned down. "Are you sure?"

"The Rangers are." TJ gave a tight, painful smile. "Keep praying, Reverend. We need this to end here before someone dies."

"You know I will."

TJ clapped Lewis on the shoulder and left.

Dr. Palmer sat on a stool facing Lewis. "Let's look at that hand, Reverend."

The doctor's touch was light but painful as he dried the hand. "Did you stick it in the flame or did something hot touch it?"

"A bit of both. Peony hid under a bed." Lewis was at a loss to explain the behavior. Then again, the young woman's childhood hadn't been like most. "When I finally coaxed her out, a piece of burning wallpaper fell on her as we were leaving. I wasn't thinking too clearly when I put it out."

"A good thing you did. She will have short hair for a while, but her scalp doesn't look any worse than a sunburn. Of course, she was much better than you about following orders and letting the others use the damp cloths to pull the heat out. I saw you passing buckets of water."

"I thought it was well enough as long as I kept the bandage around it."

"What is it with you preachers? I had to send Reverend Green home twice. The smoke isn't good for his lungs, and I can't have that cough in here." Dr. Palmer set Lewis's hand on a clean towel.

The blister had grown to the size of a silver dollar, but the painful burning had diminished. "Green's coughing blood daily."

"I know. And there isn't anything I can do about it. However, I can do something for you." Dr. Palmer went to the cupboard and took out a jar. "Carron oil is a miner's burn cure from Scotland, created by blending together limewater and linseed oil. Applied topically it helps heal burns."

Lewis memorized each instruction as the doctor bandaged his hand and forearm.

"I am going to tie you up with a sling so you won't be tempted to use that hand next time you thump a Bible. Keep it on until Monday, then come back and see me."

Nellie entered the office with a basket on her arm as he left. If he had to guess, she'd made Johnny cake and something with ham. She smiled but didn't offer him any.

An acrid smoky smell hung over the town like a mourner's cloak. The twisted stovepipe marked the grave of the cheerful yellow walls of Rose's Rescue. Scavengers would be hard pressed to find even a cook pot remaining in the blackened heap of ash and rubble. Dark scorch marks darkened the bricks on the side of the theater.

Lewis avoided breathing deeply as he passed the site while walking home to the manse.

Reverend Green sat in the parlor, with his Bible next to him on the side table. "I'm changing my sermon to the Good Samaritan. Someone needs to hear it. We can't send those women out of town while we figure out a way to continue the Rescue."

"Even if Mrs. Reese and Emily buy that abandoned hotel project, it will be some time before they can move in." Lewis sat on the bench beside him.

Reverend Green consulted his notebook. "Mrs. Reese has room for half of the women comfortably. Hannah set aside two rooms at the hotel for now. Miss Emily says they have two rooms in the new house. That still leaves us with six beds to find."

"Any vacant house they could use?"

"My place down in de Cordova is empty. But I wouldn't send those women down there. They'd be run out like everyone else."

"What about near the Springs?" Rumors about the college in the small settlement to the north moving to Dallas or Fort Worth had circulated since late spring.

"The college won't be moving for another year or two at the earliest."

The hotel would solve so many of the problems. Lewis sighed. So little he could do. "Where will they have classes? Mrs. Reese's parlor can't hold them all."

Reverend Green pointed to the window. "Let them use the church. Contrary to popular belief on both sides, it won't fall down if they meet there. Or the theater. It's empty most days. I'd say the school, but it will be back in session soon."

"You've been thinking this through."

Reverend Green closed the notebook he used for sermons. "About all I can do. Doc and the sheriff told me I had no business helping put out the fire."

"They are only concerned for your health." Lewis stifled a yawn. "If you don't mind, I'm going to take a nap."

"Make it a long one; you didn't sleep last night. I'll take care of my own dinner."

Getting undressed with one hand was more trouble than it was worth. Lewis settled for taking his boots off and idly wondered where his coat had ended up.

17

Clara sorted donated clothing on the front two pews of the church. Half of what was donated wasn't good enough for the rag sellers in Boston. Anything with usable fabric was set aside to be reworked into dresses or quilts. Reverend Green's sermon had, if nothing else, convinced Hiramsville it was time to clean out their attics.

Lewis entered with another crate in his arms. His hand was still bandaged, but he didn't wear the sling he wore in church yesterday. Hopefully it was a sign he was improving and not an indication that he was failing to follow Dr. Palmer's orders.

Her heart raced as it had when he emerged from the burning building. His injury could have been so much worse—like Jax's or Lavender's—or he might not have come out at all. The truth that she cared for him more than Catherine ever had made her chest tighten. She'd never loved someone more than she had her sister. Until now. All that mattered was that he was safe, here with her, alive. His presence brought hopeful peace that had been missing from her hectic morning.

Lewis set the crate on an empty pew. "This is the last of what was dropped off in the night. Is any of it usable?"

"You ask that as if you know much isn't." Clara embraced the normalcy of the conversation, hoping none of her emotions had shown on her face when he'd entered.

"I may be a bachelor, but I know what mold smells like. I am surprised you are not sneezing."

"A moment earlier, and you would have heard me." Clara pointed to a pile on the back pew. "I am not sure any of that is salvageable. I'd suggest burning them, but fire…"

"I could dump them through the floor of Rose's into the cave."

"Do they know how the fire started?" All she'd heard so far was speculation.

"TJ doesn't think they came through the caves. As part of the transformation from bar to refuge, they sealed off the ones to Rose's after Emily was lost in them last year. The lock on the cellar door was missing. There was a pile of debris directly below the hatch door in the kitchen."

Clara shook out a dress that was as ugly as it was serviceable. Why couldn't serviceable dresses be from pretty material? "It's hard to believe that someone wanted to burn them out."

"One theory is that the arsonist only wanted to smoke them out. The women cleaned and oiled the furniture Friday morning. That could have made the fire spread quicker."

"Or?"

"Whoever came in poured some sort of oil on the floor. GW and the other Rangers can't tell. There is so little left."

Clara held up three pairs of women's boots. Two had holes in the bottom. "Do you think we can get the bootmaker to replace the soles?"

"Will they fit someone?"

"Likely. They are near my size."

"Set them aside, and I'll go ask. Better yet, I'll get Reverend Green to. He says he isn't feeling useful. He is more likely to cajole the bootmaker into offering free services for the cost of shoe leather."

Emily entered the room with two dresses over her arms. "These were always a bit small for me. No point in moving them to the new house."

"Are they moving you today?" Clara asked.

"Trying to. If the deputy can move into the jail, that frees up another room at the hotel."

"Any word on Miss Lavender, Miss Peony, or Jax?" asked Lewis.

"Dr. Palmer let Peony leave this morning. Other than vowing to bring mobcaps back into fashion, she seems quite well. I'm sure you'll hear from her soon. It amazed her that you or anyone would come rescue her." Emily sat on the last pew and frowned. "Lavender is still under the doctor's care. The bottoms of her feet are covered with blisters. I've never seen anything so painful looking. She won't let him give her any more laudanum."

Understandable. Most of the women had been either forcibly drugged or took some form of opium in their old profession to deal with the pain of living. Clara prompted Emily to continue. "And Jax?"

Emily wiped a tear before talking. "Last night, Dr. Palmer amputated two of his fingers. GW is carrying Jax's resignation to headquarters."

"He can't be a Ranger if he is missing two fingers?" asked Clara.

"It's his gun hand." Lewis's voice was flat.

"Oh." Clara's one syllable answer was all she could get out without crying like Emily.

"Jax talked it over with GW and Doc. Said he knew he'd have to retire one day and told Doc to go ahead." Emily dabbed at her eyes again. "I should get back."

Clara hugged Emily before she left, hoping to share or lessen the grief.

Lewis sunk into the pew. "It should have been me. If I'd gone left instead of right, Jax would have a slight burn, and I'd be missing the fingers. Preachers don't need ten of them."

Clara put her hand on her hip. "Lewis Staples. Of all the stupid things to say. What if Jax couldn't coax Peony out from under the bed? They could have both died. You can't trade with him. It wasn't like you just stood around like some of the people not helping at all. Mr. Collins walked around with his notebook half the night asking people what they thought."

"He did? I didn't see him."

"It was one of those things I saw but wasn't paying attention to because I was busy." Clara sat next to Lewis. "You saved a life. You should be glad of that."

"Clara, you are good for me."

Suddenly uncomfortable with the conversation, Clara jumped up. "I better not sit for long or I'll fall asleep."

"You haven't recovered yet?"

"Mrs. Reese's is bursting. There wasn't room for me on the sleeping porch, and my room is much warmer, especially since Rae is sharing the room with me."

"I didn't think of that."

"Listen to me complaining when I have nothing but blessings." Clara pulled a worn man's shirt from the next box and added it to the rag pile.

"I'll be off then. Other than the boots, is there anything you need?"

"Usable donations?"

"I'll pray for some."

She watched Lewis go. He was good for her too. Why hadn't she let him continue with what he'd been saying?

She looked up at the stained-glass window for answers. A conversation could have led to the kiss they hadn't been able to have before the fire. But she wanted the first kiss inside of a church with any man to be because she married him there. Otherwise kissing in a church felt utterly improper.

Not that it mattered, at the moment. There was far too much to do. The women needed clothing and necessities. She needed to use her energy to help them, not worry about her own miniscule problems.

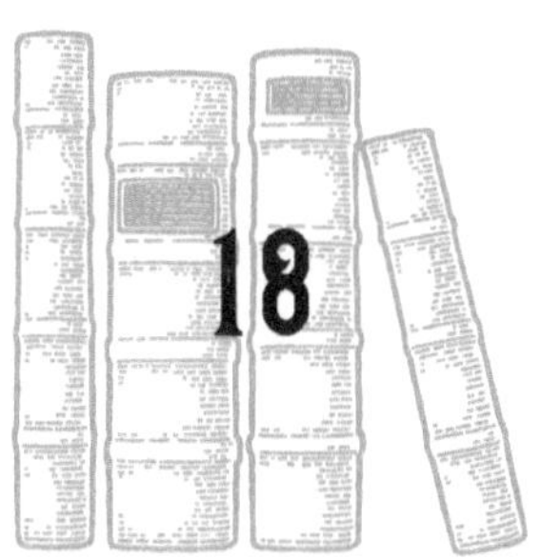

18

ill you fetch me the red leather-bound volume of sermons?" asked Reverend Green.

The collar Lewis wore felt more like one belonging to a canine than a minister. With his hand bandaged and the mutual decision that he shouldn't preach, Lewis had little to do. Even the cooking and cleaning chores had been delegated to others. Fetching a book, walking around town waving at people, and offering a smile comprised his current lot.

Lewis found the book in question among Reverend Green's things which had taken over much of the office. Considering Lewis's collection of books numbered twenty, there was more than enough room.

"Here you go." Lewis set the book on the table next to Reverend Green's favorite chair.

"You should study. Write a few sermons that you can fall back on."

"I can study, but even I can't read what I write with my left hand."

Reverend Green tapped his forehead. "Write it up here. You'll remember it when you need to."

"Mind if I borrow a book?"

"Go ahead. They'll all be yours someday. May as well figure out which ones you want to keep now."

"I wish you wouldn't talk like that."

"Stating a fact? I am dying. The pneumonia I had last winter nearly killed me and left my lungs in a terrible state. Isn't anything anyone can do. Dr. Palmer said I might live longer in a drier climate. I am too old to start over someplace else. De Cordova was supposed to bring me some rest, but I spent too much time wondering when someone was going to kick me and my little garden out of the area. Doc says working isn't good for me."

"Since your return, there has been nothing but worries to deal with."

"Yes, but I am not alone. Sharing a burden helps. That is the one thing I've missed the most about not having my wife around."

The few minutes Lewis had talked to Clara helped him clear his mind as well, although there were many problems larger than either of them to focus on.

Lewis settled down with a particularly dogeared text and read.

Heavy footfalls on the porch preceded a loud knock. Lewis glanced through the screen door and froze. Reverend Whitesides stood outside. Lewis set aside his book and rose. As he walked to the door, he tapped Reverend Green on his shoulder. The wide eyes of his friend showed he hadn't expected the minister from Austin either.

Lewis opened the door. "Come in. Were we expecting you?"

"I assume you were, considering the letter the two of you sent three weeks ago. The addition of the fire and newspaper articles mailed to us guaranteed it, don't you think?"

Reverend Green stood, leaving the comfortable chair for their visitor. "Well, yes, we simply didn't know when."

"I find it is best, in cases like this, not to send out a warning." Reverend Whitesides gestured for Reverend Green to take his previous chair, and he settled himself in the one Lewis had vacated. He nodded at Lewis's bound hand. "I assume that is the burn you received while rescuing the woman from the fire?"

Lewis looked at his bandage. "How did you know about that?"

"I walked through the town from the train station. A young boy told me what a hero you were, and valiantly defended you against the newspaper's innuendos."

The boy must have been Donny. Unsure if an answer or defense were needed, Lewis waited for someone else to say something.

"Will you be staying the night?" asked Reverend Green.

"If I may."

"Would you like something to drink while I prepare the room?" Lewis's room to be exact. There was only one furnished bedroom upstairs.

"That would be nice." Reverend Whitesides set the hat he still carried on the table beside him.

Lewis should have asked to hang up his hat. One would think his mother hadn't taught him any manners. He scooped up the hat on his way to the kitchen.

Changing bed linens with one hand took three times as long as normal. Lewis looked around his room for anything he didn't want the senior minister to find. Letters from Catherine, which should be disposed of anyway, his letter to Clara when he thought she'd eloped. Letters from his mother. He couldn't remember what was in each one, but certainly more than he wanted Reverend Whitesides learning. Lewis tucked them all into his old satchel and slid it into the space between the wall and the wardrobe. It was that or carry it down to his office. Lewis stopped at the door. Since he would be sleeping on the couch, the office would be a better place.

With his good hand, he tried to fish the satchel out of its hiding place, a feat that required more agility than he possessed, and the satchel only moved further behind the wardrobe. Retrieving it required moving the piece of furniture. Reverend Whitesides was unlikely to go to such lengths.

Lewis carried the soiled sheets downstairs and put them in a basket on the back porch for one of the women from the Rescue to collect and wash. The reverends were debating a passage in Isaiah. Reverend Whitesides looked up when Lewis entered the room. "Finished? Why don't we take a walk?"

Lewis held open the door and then fell into step with the older man.

"Reverend Green tells me you are courting the twin sister of the woman you were engaged to."

The pause begged for a response. "Yes, I am."

"Have you proposed yet?"

"Yes, and I was turned down. We have since talked about it."

"Why did she turn you down?"

"Because I asked for the wrong reasons."

"And what were those?"

"The same reason I proposed to her sister last year: I was told I needed a wife." If the church hadn't pressured him to propose, he might have asked Clara to write him for a year and proposed by mail when the time was right. Or he might have eventually succumbed to one of the marriage-minded mamas and courted a girl from the congregation. Although none of them interested him.

Reverend Whitesides slowed his step. "You do."

"Not at the expense of having a real marriage."

"What do you mean?"

"I can't marry a woman just to keep a job. We teach that a husband and wife should be equally yoked and be helpmates. If I am marrying for the sake of a job, it is for the wrong reason."

"Do you want to marry her?"

"More than anyone I've ever met."

"Then why don't you?"

"Because I hurt her, and she needs to be able to trust me. Saying I love you isn't enough."

"So if I demote you in the morning, what will you do?"

"Be the best clerk I can be." Until that moment, Lewis hadn't been sure he could be a clerk. He would, if that was his only path back into the ministry and Clara's trust.

"You wouldn't propose?"

"Not right now. I do want to marry her, and I will, when the timing is right. When I have her father's permission. Even if you demote me to a clerk or dismiss me, I will propose."

Reverend Whitesides walked several steps without talking.

Lewis kept his eyes on his feet.

They turned back to the manse. "I'll let you know my decision in the morning."

Lewis left Reverend Whitesides at the door and continued on his walk. It would be so easy to walk to Mrs. Reese's and find Clara. No. He wouldn't. He needed to write to Mr. Taylor. It would take nearly two weeks to get an answer. If only his right hand were healed.

⟨⟩◈⟨⟩

Becky carried the pan of rolls to the table. "Guess who Donny saw get off the train last night?"

Clara wiped her brow. She'd been awake since before dawn and was far too tired to play guessing games. "One of the Rangers?"

"No." Becky looked expectantly at Clara.

"I don't know that many people, how can I guess whom it might be?"

"Reverend Whitesides. He asked dozens of questions. Donny told him Lewis was a hero."

"From Austin?" Had Lewis lost his job? It was her fault. Why hadn't he come by?

"Yup, all the way from Austin. Spent the night at the manse."

"What else did Donny say?" Clara clasped her hands together to keep them from shaking.

"Only that he left on the morning train."

"Who left?"

"Reverend Whitesides."

"Alone? Not with Lewis?"

"Yup. Doesn't mean that Lewis won't take the evening train." Becky's observation was far less than helpful.

Clara looked around the large kitchen. Perhaps she could get away if she delivered some of the food to the women who had taken up residence in Emily's new home. Nellie had packed the baskets for the doctor's office, Emily's, and one for someone else. "Nellie, where is the small basket going?"

"It's for the reverends. With Reverend Staples's hand bound and Reverend Green not being a good cook, I made one for them."

"I'll deliver the one to Emily, if it will help."

"It would be better if you could take the basket to Doc's." Nellie pushed the basket across the table. "Lavender and Jax are eating enough for six or seven people. Doc said sometimes burn victims do."

If she took the long way back from the doctor's office, it would put her within sight of the church—close enough that if Lewis were outside, she could talk with him without raising suspicions. Clara picked up the basket, surprised by its weight. "So you packed enough food for fifteen?"

"Almost. You may want to take the laundry wagon."

"I think I can manage."

"Good. Then I'll take the wagon and drop off the clothing at the hotel." Nellie picked up the other baskets and headed for the back door.

Halfway to Dr. Palmer's, Clara wished she hadn't been so quick to turn down the use of the wagon. She passed the jail and the newspaper office. The press clanked. The Wednesday paper must be late.

Clara put the food away in Dr. Palmer's kitchen, and then went upstairs to check on Lavender and Jax. Peony sat reading to Lavender, so she only waved her hellos. Jax's door was closed. Clara said a silent prayer for his recovery before leaving the office.

On her way back home, Mr. Collins was standing outside of the newspaper office, selling copies of the day's news. "Miss Taylor, would you like a copy?"

"I'm sorry, I don't have any money with me. I was only delivering food to the doctor's office." Clara tried to step around the paper he held in front of her.

"You should read it."

"I am sure I will."

"Complimentary." Mr. Collins plopped a copy into the empty basket.

"Thank you." Clara nodded and walked on. A bold headline in the bottom corner caught her eye.

Church Leadership Visits Hiramsville

Preacher Gets his Comeuppance

As much as she wanted to read more, Clara wasn't going to give Mr. Collins the satisfaction of reading the paper where he could watch her reaction.

Clara turned to cross the square. Perfect timing. Lewis walked toward her.

As he got closer, he tucked a paper into his coat. "Good morning, Clara."

"Good morning. How do you do?" There were enough people around, she didn't dare ask more.

"Having a lovely day. And you? Has your day been pleasant?"

"Yes. I just delivered food to Dr. Palmer's."

"I need to post a letter, then I can escort you to your destination."

Clara smiled. "Of course."

She walked with Lewis into the post office and waited against the wall. Lewis spoke quietly to the postmaster while he paid for the postage. As he turned away, the postmaster tilted his head and winked at Clara. Odd. Clara waved her hand in a silent greeting.

Lewis held the door for her as they left.

Clara looked over her shoulder to see the postmaster smile and wave again. He wasn't usually so friendly.

"Do you have time to walk down by the river?" asked Lewis.

"If we aren't too long."

As soon as they were out of the square, questions burst out of Clara. "Becky said your superiors were here. Even the paper printed about it. What happened?"

"The newspaper?"

Clara handed Lewis the paper. "Mr. Collins gave me a copy. I am sure it is because he wanted me to read the article about you."

Lewis read the article out loud.

"Tuesday evening, Reverend Whitesides answered letters from many Hiramsville residents. Some observed a conversation where our own young reverend appeared to be downcast. Residents wonder if the next church social will be his farewell."

"Is that all?"

"Yes. Hardly newsworthy."

Clara clenched her hands. "Are you leaving?"

"I don't know."

"Did he give you an ultimatum?" His short answers were so frustrating.

They started down the riverside trail. Clara decided to wait until Lewis spoke rather than press him for answers he seemed unready to give. They watched the river in silence.

The sound of the water tumbling calmed Lewis's heart. While he hoped to have a chance to speak with Clara today, meeting her as he was posting a letter to her father was poor timing. For a moment, he'd feared the postmaster would say something to give his intention away.

When they reached their log, Lewis took Clara's hand and sat down. "There isn't an easy answer to your questions. Yes, Reverend Whitesides was here because of the newspapers and letters he'd received, including reports from myself and Reverend Green. As far as the newspaper article, no one is planning a farewell social yet."

"So what did he say?"

"In regard to me staying?"

"Of course." Clara's lips thinned.

"Only that I'd given him something to ponder, and he needed to discuss my situation with others."

"What does that mean for your job? For us?"

"For now, we will keep courting."

Clara searched his face, her brows still worried.

As he gazed into her eyes, Lewis's heart beat faster. He wanted to tell her how much she meant to him, how he would give up his job for her, and that together things would work out. He wasn't ready to say those things, yet. Maybe by the time her father replied, the words would be there.

Instead, he lifted her hand to his lips and pressed a kiss to her palm while keeping his eyes locked on hers. He poured all of his emotions into the moment. He wanted her to feel how much he cared for her, how much he valued her influence in his life.

In that moment, Lewis felt a sense of peace wash over him. He knew that he didn't have to say anything to express his feelings. As he lowered their hands, he saw the love and understanding in Clara's eyes and knew that she had felt it too.

Softly, she smiled. "Was that to distract me from worrying so much?"

"A little." Lewis smiled. "Also to reassure me that you still like me."

"Oh, Lewis." Clara jumped up. "I'm beginning to understand why our mothers complained about our fathers."

His grin widened as he stood. "So you are still courting me?"

She put her hand on her hip and blew out a puff of air. "If we aren't, you better stop kissing me like that."

If only he dared kiss her as he wanted to. Yet if a simple kiss on the hand provoked her so much, she may not be ready for more. "I intend to keep kissing you, so we are still courting."

At Clara's gasp, he offered his arm and walked her home. With any luck, her father would respond with a telegram soon, and he could kiss her the way he wanted to.

Dr. Palmer rewrapped Lewis's hand. "Your prayers must be working. Your hand is much better than I expected after five days of healing. Has it been five days? It is Thursday, isn't it?"

"Yes. It is." Lewis didn't comment on the gray circles under the doctor's eyes. How are Jax and Miss Lavender?"

"I'd tell you to go see for yourself, but my guess is Miss Lavender has no less than three visitors in her room. Those women are keeping her mind occupied while she heals. The burns on her feet will keep her from walking for a while. And Jax is sleeping." Dr. Palmer cleaned off the tray he'd used while changing Lewis's bandage. "I had to remove another finger yesterday."

"How did he take the news?"

"I'm not sure. He is far too stoic. Pray for him."

"I will." Lewis took his leave of the doctor's office. In the distance, the train whistled. The mail would be here soon.

A crowd had already formed on the walkway in front of the post office. Lewis waited for the mail clerk to sort the packages and letters that had arrived on the afternoon train. Finally, the clerk called out his name, and Lewis stepped forward.

The postmaster handed him a single, thin letter from his mother. The second one this week. Mother never wrote more than once. Outside of the post office, he looked for a private place to read. Others, intent on the day's mail, greeted him as they passed. Workers shouted at each other as they hauled away the debris from Rose's. Sitting on the bench that used to be by the door wasn't an option. Privacy in the square would be impossible to find.

The door to the church stood open. Donations to the Rescue had been sorted and cleared, leaving the building empty. Lewis sat on a side pew near the window. He paused a moment before opening the letter, steeling himself for what he might find inside. Lewis slowly unfolded the letter and read. His mother's handwriting was neat as always, but her words were heavy in his heart.

> Mr. Taylor returned from New York City without locating Catherine or proof that she has eloped. He found no explanation for her disappearance. There is nothing left to do but accept that she is simply gone.

A wave of sadness washed over him. He bore some of the blame for Catherine's actions. Had he been honest about the proposal mistake, would she have never sought a way out through an illicit relationship? He had ruined three lives that day. If only he had apologized then.

Clara. Did she know yet? Last week, she'd received a letter from Catherine. Perhaps she held the clue to finding her sister. Lewis tucked the letter into his jacket pocket and set out for Mrs. Reese's home. There was no telling where he might find Clara.

Two large tents stood in the backyard. It was both a practical solution for the need of shelter and a place to meet.

The women nodded and gave their hellos as he wandered through the maze of industry. Clara cut fabric squares in the second tent.

"I see you are putting those scraps to good use."

Clara smiled and returned to her cutting. "They have already finished two quilts. The shop in Fort Worth sent a new sewing machine and a used one. We are working rapidly to replace everything we can."

"Is there a place to talk privately?"

Clara looked at the house. "Not here. Even the attic is in use."

"Can you take a short walk? I've had a letter from my mother."

"Yes." Clara set down her scissors. "Becky, if anyone needs me, I'll be back in a few minutes."

Becky looked up from the pile of scraps she sorted. "Take your time."

They took the path by the river to the same fallen tree they'd sat on last week.

Clara turned to him. "Tell me and be quick. Bad news should not be drawn out."

"Your father went to New York. He returned without finding Catherine." The words hovered in the air like a heavy weight.

"I knew something was—" Her voice cracked, and she struggled to keep her composure. "Her letter last week was cryptic, even for her."

He stepped forward and reached out to take her hands in his, squeezing them as if he could take away all of her sorrow. Her hands trembled in his grasp. Tears pooled in her eyes as she processed the news, and her face crumpled in grief.

"I'm so sorry, Clara," Lewis said, his heart aching with sympathy. He pulled her into an embrace, and she melted into his arms, allowing the tears to come. He let her cry until she no longer could, then spoke softly. "We will find her. I know we will."

Clara looked up at him and nodded, wiping away her tears with a lace-edged handkerchief. "You know my sister. We won't unless she wants to be found. Did your mother say if Father hired the Pinkertons?"

"No."

"I should see if I have any letters. Perhaps she will have written again."

"Did she say where she was in her last letter?"

"She talked of Niagara Falls. I already knew they were going there." She turned to face him. "Is my face presentable?"

Lewis wiped the remainder of a tear with the pad of his thumb. "You're beautiful."

Clara smiled weakly and pressed a kiss into his palm.

He stood frozen for a moment at her act of affection. Not wanting to ruin anything by speaking, he held out his arm. She laced her hand through his elbow, and they took the path back to the square.

⟨•◇•⟩

A single letter in her mother's handwriting waited for Clara. She handed it to Lewis. "I cannot bear to read it. Will you?"

"Are you sure?" asked Lewis.

Fear overwhelmed her. What if they did find Catherine and she wasn't alive? Reading the words would be too painful. "Yes."

"Out loud?"

"No." She took his arm and walked to the river path and back to the log.

Lewis broke the seal and opened the letter. His eyes scanned across the page and widened. Quickly, he folded the letter and thrust it at her. "I don't think I was the one who should have read this."

"More bad news?"

"Nothing you haven't heard before." The tips of his ears turned red.

Clara smoothed the letter out.

> . . . *Your father located Bernard and his family at their Fifth Avenue home along with Bernard's fiancée, another member of New York's elite. In a private conversation, Bernard denied knowing where Catherine might be. Father pressed him as to the paternity of Catherine's child and was tossed out of the house. The Pinkertons were somewhat more successful in discovering that Bernard had been on a holiday for three weeks. Your father has engaged their services.*
>
> *As for you, we are most anxious about your welfare. I have yet to receive your reply to our letter asking if you were to wed Lewis or return home. Since there has been no cable informing us of your return date, I can only assume you are already wed, or intend to soon . . .*

Clara's cheeks heated, and she folded up the letter. "Mother won't be pleased when she receives my letter, will she?"

Lewis sat next to her. "They only want to know you are safe."

"In that case, the letter I sent regarding the fire may cause her to become completely unhinged."

"Revered Green wrote my letter." Lewis held up his right hand. "Our mothers will be quite worried."

"Is it wrong that I take comfort that we are too far away for them to appear one afternoon and take us to task?"

Lewis covered his left ear with his hand. "My ear hurts at the thought."

"My parents will have to content themselves with the knowledge that you are courting me and I have no other suitors."

"What about Dr. Palmer?"

"We spoke Sunday afternoon when I took over some food. He is a fine man." The next words didn't come as easy. She'd never fully declared herself to a man. All the novels in the world didn't prepare her to say what she needed. She looked Lewis in the eyes as she spoke. "My heart lies elsewhere."

He blinked. Not the reaction she hoped for. Clara looked away.

With a single finger he lifted her chin. The gesture was both tender and bold, and the sensation it created was unfamiliar, yet surprisingly pleasant. As soon as she met his eyes, his hand dropped and intertwined with hers as they had at the theater.

"With me?" His soft words filled with the wonder she felt.

The only sound was the soft ripple of the river. Clara's mouth dried up, so she nodded.

Lewis slowly brought her hand up to his mouth and placed a gentle kiss upon her knuckles. The warmth of his lips' touch spread through her. He never took his intense gaze from hers as if searching for a reaction. Nervously, she licked her lips.

Lewis leaned in and brushed his lips against hers softly. At his touch, Clara felt the world melt away. He pulled back a mere space of a breath.

"That should have been our first kiss."

Each word danced across her cheek like the breeze of a butterfly wing. His lips touched hers again, longer, warmer. He ended before the kiss took on the intensity of the day of her arrival, yet this one held more meaning. It was as if his heart spoke to hers the words she still needed to hear from him. Words she dared not speak herself.

He raised his hand to cup her cheek. Clara leaned into his touch.

"I wish this had been our first kiss so you might know it was only for you. You are the one I love, the one I always loved."

Her emotions leaked over into her eyes.

"What did I say wrong?" A hint of alarm tinged Lewis's voice as he lowered his hand.

Blinking back tears, Clara hunted for his hand, their connection. Unable to find it, she laid her hand on his chest. "Nothing. You said nothing wrong."

"But, you're crying..." An unsaid again ended his sentence.

"They are joyful tears." Clara brought her hand to his cheek. She leaned in, and he met her in their next kiss.

This time the kiss was not gentle nor soft. It held all their emotions—worry and hope, love and longing. As they parted, Clara's heart swelled in her chest, and she knew that nothing would ever be the same. Though they had no formal understanding, she was his and he was hers.

In the moment they shared, something changed. Gone was the cloud of unspoken words that had hung between them.

The realization brought fresh tears to Clara's eyes, but this time it was a mix of joy and relief. Lewis looked at her with an expression of pure adoration. "I love you, Clara."

Clara smiled through her tears and whispered back, "I love you too, Lewis."

lenching and unclenching his hand to loosen the muscles that had been bound for two weeks, Lewis hurried to a meeting of the board of directors of Rose's Rescue. To his relief, Dr. Palmer declared Lewis's severely burned hand healed enough to shed the bandages.

The town would take much longer to recover from the tragedy. A black scar blotted the corner of the square where the building that housed Rose's Rescue had stood for so many years. A stark reminder of what hatred could do. TJ was no closer to catching the arsonist.

The sweltering August heat did little to calm tempers as the newspaper continued to print pieces about Rose's women or, as the last column dubbed them, the Bruised Buds. Lewis fumed when he first read the moniker. Sadly, he now heard it in conversations as he passed through town. As for him, the articles no longer mentioned the church and its ministers.

After Reverend Whitesides's visit, Lewis's name no longer appeared in the paper, and direct criticism of Lewis ended. But that did not stop others from whispering behind his back when he walked past. They had found no notes at the church or parsonage since the fire. Reverend Green speculated Lewis's relationship with Clara put an end to any speculation of Lewis courting anyone else.

Lewis ran up the stairs to the church. Mrs. Reese, Emily, Hannah, Clara, and Reverend Green already sat near the open window.

"Sorry I'm late. Dr. Palmer had another patient to see first." Lewis held up his hand.

"You only missed the prayer." Reverend Green's eyes twinkled. "As I recall, it was your turn for the invocation."

Lewis sat on the bench next to Clara.

Emily opened a notebook. "I am unsure if I should start with the slightly bad news, the bad news, the terrible news, or the hopeful news first."

"I always prefer to be hopeful," said Reverend Green.

"We heard from the developer. The lowered price he has put on the hotel property is reasonable. Unfortunately, the price is a thousand dollars more than we have. He gave us until the first of September to raise the funds. I have no idea how we can raise such an amount in less than four weeks. A loan is out of the question since we can't use a pile of ashes as collateral."

"We could rebuild at the old location for less." Mrs. Reese sighed. "However, Rose's was full to bursting, and we know there are more women who seek the safety we offer. That is why we were looking at the hotel in the first place."

"Next on the list," Emily continued. "Two of our friends have left the Rescue. One has accepted a proposal of marriage, and the other only said she was taking the train west." Emily paused for a moment.

Lewis assumed they were all thinking the same things and even praying that their new lives would be unlike their former ones.

"As far as classes, I've talked to all the women. They are not comfortable with meeting here in the church. Some fear that whoever burned them out would do the same here. Others have an understandable aversion to churches in general. I haven't found a place with a room big enough that will allow us to rent. We are taking a holiday from classes while we try to replace lost clothing and orders." Emily tapped her notebook. "Housing continues to be a problem. However, even with three or more to a room, most women prefer to stay together at Mrs. Reese's. I think that covers the main points. Suggestions?"

"If we were in Boston, I'd suggest holding a society benefit to raise the funds," said Clara. "Of course, that would take months to organize."

Emily shook her head. "We held an event last spring. It was poorly attended. Even if every adult in town came to something, we couldn't charge them ten dollars apiece when a dollar would be considered a stretch for some."

"I suppose you've approached all of the businesses in town as well?" Clara didn't look very hopeful.

"Every business in the county," said Reverend Green.

Lewis had no new ideas to offer. "I suppose the restaurant wouldn't be feasible now. Not that it would earn a thousand dollars in a month."

Mrs. Reese turned and stared, as did Hannah. One of the plans offered if the hotel could be purchased was to turn Rose's into a restaurant where graduates could work and live.

Reverend Green leaned forward. "Years ago, when towns were growing faster than we could build, I saw restaurants and even bars housed in tents. Is the foundation sturdy enough that we could put a tent there and have a restaurant?"

"Most of the foundation has been torn up. The kitchen area is open to the cave below," said Lewis.

"Still smells of smoke. No one wants to eat in a place that smells like that." Hannah's observation was too true.

"I'd set it up in my yard, but the neighbors are commenting on the tents I have up for the women to sew and work in," said Mrs. Reese.

Emily sighed. "I couldn't think of anything either. Other than the need to purchase food and pay Clara, we don't have any expenses. Both are necessary."

"I'm not. With no classroom or books. I am not contributing much. I have some money to pay for my board." Clara looked at Mrs. Reese. "—which I have yet to be charged."

"And you won't be." Mrs. Reese's declaration left no room for argument.

"You should at least take the pay owed you," pressed Emily.

"If you pay it, I'll turn around and put the entire sum in the donation fund." Clara raised her chin.

Emily wrote in her book. "Well, we are forty dollars closer to our goal. Thank you, Clara."

"Which doesn't fix anything, does it?" asked Clara.

"No." Emily's disheartening answer was as blunt as it was true.

"At home, our church was always collecting for foreign missions or other things. What if we wrote to our families or to Bradford College alumni? The concept would appeal to them, and as someone pointed out, almost everyone likes the concept of the Rescue, they just don't like it next door."

"I could send letters to my friends who serve in more affluent congregations." Reverend Green paused to cough. "I will also write the leadership."

"I have a few contacts as well." Few, as in Lewis could count them on one hand.

"We need to get writing. The more letters we can have in tomorrow morning's mail pouch the better," said Hannah.

Lewis's hand ached at the thought.

Clara glanced down at his hand. "Several of the women have beautiful handwriting. If we draft a letter, they could make copies, then we would only need to add a personal note."

"Excellent." Emily snapped her ledger shut. "The reverends and I can draft a letter. Clara, will you go to the mercantile and buy enough paper for fifty letters?"

"Make that sixty. I have some friends too," said Hannah.

Clara stood. "Do we have enough pens and ink?"

"There are plenty at the manse," said Reverend Green.

"I have several that have been left at the hotel." Hannah also stood. "I need to get back there before the afternoon train comes in. Friday's train is always good for an extra customer or two."

Lewis didn't ask if she would have room with some of the women still rooming there. Hannah would tell him she did, even if she had to sleep on a cot in the kitchen.

"I'll round up volunteers to write. We will have to rearrange the dining room so they can have a table. Every inch of Mrs. Reese's is covered with some project or other." Clara hurried out of the door.

Lewis glanced at Clara's empty seat. Most of their days since the fire had gone the same with neither of them having enough time for more than a short evening stroll.

⟡

Coming out of the mercantile with every piece of stationary Mr. Tarr carried, Clara stopped abruptly.

It had to be a mirage.

People saw things that didn't exist in the heat didn't they? Catherine would never be seen so disheveled in public. Her hair was out of place, her face the color of a dust bin, and her condition clearly evident.

"You look at me as if I am a ghost."

At the sound of her sister's voice, Clara's limbs found their strength. "Catherine?"

"Of course, you goose." Catherine opened her arms for Clara's embrace as if it were the only logical thing to do after a month of who knew what.

Adjusting her parcel of papers, Clara managed a half hug. Even with the evidence overwhelming her senses, Clara couldn't believe her twin was here. She pulled back. "Do Mother and Father know where you are?"

"Why would they?"

Clara walked her sister toward the hotel. There was no other private place to sit nearby. "Father hired the Pinkertons."

"Why?"

"He went to New York and talked to Bernard."

"Oh." Catherine's shoulders lowered.

Clara held the door open for her sister. Hannah stood behind the counter, and her eyes widened.

"Hannah, do you have an empty room?"

"Why can't I stay with you and Lewis?" Catherine's voice took on a whine Clara hadn't heard in months.

At Hannah's positive reply, Clara pulled two dollars from her purse. "Three days?"

"Miss Clara, you know you—"

Clara put her hand up to stop Hannah's refusal. "Hannah, this is my sister, Catherine. She will be a paying customer."

From the pigeonholes behind her, Hannah took a key. "204 is next to the bathroom. Do you have any trunks?"

Catherine looked around. "I left mine at the station."

Hannah nodded. "If you have your ticket stubs, I'll find someone to deliver them to your room."

Clara set her parcel on the counter. "I hate to impose, but could you see these get sent over to Mrs. Reese and tell her I'll be there as soon as possible?"

"Of course." Hannah set the parcel of paper on her desk. "Would you like me to send Rae up with something cool to drink?"

"Please, and do add it to Catherine's bill." Clara turned to her sister. "Let's get you settled in."

"I don't understand why I can't stay with you and Lewis."

Hannah gave Clara a sympathetic look as Clara herded her sister upstairs.

Blue and yellow daisies sprinkled the wallpaper. Matching blue curtains and quilt gave the room a cheery feel.

Catherine sunk onto the bed. "I didn't expect something so nice in the middle of Texas."

"I didn't think I'd find you wandering about town, so we are both astonished." Clara removed her hat pin and set her hat on the dressing table. Before she could ask any of the dozens of questions she had, a knock sounded on the door.

Rae stood in the hallway with a tray. "I added some biscuits."

Clara took it from her and smiled. "Thank you. I'll introduce you later."

Until she knew what was going on, she wanted to keep the speculation and gossip to a minimum.

Clara poured a tumblerful of lemonade and gave it to her sister before pouring a smaller one for herself. "I am bursting with questions. Why are you here?"

"Because I had nowhere else to go."

"Mother wrote you aren't married. What happened?"

"I met Bernard as planned. We took a train to Niagara Falls. When we arrived, it was too late in the day to get married. One disaster followed another, and we kept missing the clerk who was to get us our marriage license. We spent several blissful days together." Catherine sipped her drink.

Clara waited patiently for Catherine to continue. Silence was her best tool.

"Our last night, he went out to get our dinner. He didn't want me to walk too far. He brought back a bottle of whiskey and drank the whole thing. I'd never seen him drink before. He said all manner of nasty things about you and me. Then he informed me that his family would never accept me and our child, nor would they believe that he was the father. He dropped fifty dollars on the bed and left." Tears formed in Catherine's eyes. "I knew he would come back. I waited and waited until the manager came and informed me that I needed to leave."

Clara sipped her lemonade and waited for more. There was always more.

"I didn't know where to go or what to do. I figured, by now, you and Lewis had told Mother and Father the truth. I could never go back to Boston. Bernard suggested I visit a doctor. I thought it was to see if the baby was healthy. I am expanding ever so fast. But the doctor was a...a..." Catherine rested a hand on her expanding middle. "I ran out of that office as soon as I realized. I've made a lot of mistakes, but I couldn't do that."

"I went to New York and found a boarding house and wrote Bernard. I waited for him to come for me. I was running out of money. So I sold my wedding dress and my finer gowns. The woman who ran the place realized I didn't really have a husband and kicked me out."

"So you were in New York when Father was looking for you?" asked Clara.

Catherine shrugged. "I don't know. I never saw him. I never saw anyone. I went to Bernard's address. His father was there. He asked me so many questions. He sent a servant to purchase passage on the train to Texas and gave me ten dollars for food. Once I arrived I was supposed to wire him, and he will send me a thousand dollars. Then another thousand after a doctor confirms that I had the child. I had to sign so many papers. I can never contact Bernard again once I have the money."

Only the thought that things could have been much worse kept Clara from reacting.

"Then, I thought, since you must be married by now, that I could come and take your teaching position. I could continue to be you."

"You cannot be me. Because I am me. And Lewis and I aren't married."

"What do you mean, you aren't married? You said you would marry Lewis so he wouldn't lose his position. I had everything arranged." Catherine's voice grew louder with each word. A particular glint came into her twin's eyes. One all too familiar. Catherine was plotting. "If you're not married to him, then he can marry me. We never formally broke our proposal."

Clara closed her eyes and silently prayed for wisdom. If only her sister had shown up before she had accepted Lewis's suit and they acknowledged their feelings. Could she give up Lewis again? He had yet to propose. Although they did have an understanding of sorts, didn't they? They'd kissed several times now.

Pressure grew in Clara's chest. It was the same feeling she'd felt the previous summer when Lewis had proposed to Catherine. This time it was ten times worse. Perhaps it was because her heart had only begun to heal and wasn't strong yet. Mrs. Reese would tell her to fight for her chance at love. How could she? If Catherine married Lewis, the baby would have a father. The thought twisted deep into Clara's heart.

Clara took another deep breath before speaking. "When I arrived, I realized I couldn't lie to him and everyone. He has only begun to court me."

"Court you? Why would he need to do that? You have followed him around like a lost puppy dog since you could walk, or since he danced with you at our coming out ball. You have talked of no one else. Even Bernard knew you didn't admire him as much as you did some preacher who left behind his family's money."

"I don't think you will understand." Her sister never understood how Clara could be content without dozens of friends.

"Since you are not married yet, he must not be that enamored with you. Then there is a chance that he might…" Catherine's words trailed off.

Clara stood before she let her emotions win and she started yelling at her sister. "I must get going."

"Where? You can't just leave me here."

"I was in the middle of some very important errands. I thought you might appreciate a nap and a chance to wash up."

"Where is Lewis?"

Clara forced out a truthful answer that was still a lie. "I don't know his schedule."

"I must go see him."

"Perhaps it is better if you rest first. Though some color has returned to your face, you still look as if…"

"The cat dragged me in?"

"I wouldn't have said it that way."

"You are right. It wouldn't do for Lewis to see me like this. Where are my trunks?"

"It may take a while for Hannah to have them delivered."

Catherine came over and checked her reflection in the mirror. "I am a sight. Bernard's father only got me a second-class ticket. I had to sit and sleep on benches the whole way here. I rubbed dirt on my face so men would ignore me."

That explained the dishevelment. Lavender would be impressed by her twin's ingenuity in protecting herself.

"I'll be back in an hour or so."

"Don't go." Catherine clutched Clara's free hand.

"I won't be too long." Or she wouldn't be gone long enough. Clara wrenched her hand from her sister's grip.

Clara hurried downstairs. Hannah spoke with a young man Clara recognized as one who often did odd jobs around the hotel.

Clara waited for them to finish before she spoke to Hannah. "I need some time to deal with things. I'm not asking for you to lie or anything, but if my sister's trunks could be delayed as long as possible..."

Hannah laughed. "That can be arranged. Will an hour be enough?"

"I hope so."

Clara stopped at the station to send a telegraph to her parents.

> Twin arrived safely.
> Need guidance.
> Clara

Now she needed to inform Lewis. He should be at Mrs. Reese's by now.

21

ewis cut the potatoes and added them to the stew as the parishioner's note had indicated. After dinner, he'd go to write his letters. If they were quick, he might finally get more than five minutes with Clara. He wanted to propose, and this time for the right reasons. He'd sent off a letter, dictated to Reverend Green a week ago Monday. If Mr. Taylor replied quickly, a return letter could have arrived by now. Lewis's heart wouldn't wait for another week. Considering the letters Clara received—

A knock on the front door interrupted his thoughts. Reverend Green's soft footfalls indicated he would answer and deal with whatever request was being made.

A moment later, Reverend Green stuck his head in the kitchen. "You have a visitor. I would have asked that she wait outside, but the porch is still in full sun, so I invited her into the parlor. Would you like me to stay?"

The offer only had one answer, especially if this woman was unmarried. "Please do." Lewis rinsed and dried his hands.

The woman stood with her back to him looking out of the window. With her hat still on her head, she looked remarkably like Clara. Only Clara hadn't worn a bustle to anything other than church services for weeks. She wouldn't have changed her clothes since this afternoon. Lewis cleared his throat.

The woman turned.

"Catherine?"

"Surprise." Her right hand rested on the swelling at her waist.

There was no mistaking she was with child. She didn't wear a ring on her left hand, though he'd noticed that several of the women in his congregation removed their rings during the latter half of their pregnancy. He feared he knew the answer to the question, but he asked anyway. "Where is your husband?"

"Bernard refused to marry me."

The next question needed to be asked even if Lewis dreaded the answer. "Why are you here?"

"Isn't it obvious? You are my fiancé after all."

"I believe you jilted me."

"Not formally."

"You eloped and sent Clara in your place. There is no other conclusion than you broke off the engagement."

Catherine sat in a chair and pushed out her lower lip in a pout he knew all too well. Clara never pouted. Clara was also correct; it was nearly impossible to think of them without comparing.

"You didn't marry her. So our engagement must still be in effect."

Reverend Green snorted and coughed.

Catherine turned to the noise and glared. "Does he need to be in here?"

"Yes, he does."

Her lip jutted out further. "We are old friends and engaged. We hardly need a chaperone."

"We are not engaged." Lewis stood as far from her chair as possible. "It is best that Reverend Green remains here."

Catherine huffed and turned her full attention back to Lewis. "If you marry me, all our problems will be solved. You will no longer be on probation or whatever it is that you are subject to as an unwed minister. And my child will have the most excellent of fathers."

"I can't marry you."

"Why? Have you gone and made my sister a promise?" Catherine pulled a fan out. From the need to cool herself or because she wanted to flirt, he couldn't tell. "She didn't mention anything other than you were courting."

"My relationship with your sister is between Clara and me." Where was Clara? If Donny were around, he'd send the boy running.

"Do you love her? Of course you do. I see the blush on your cheeks. She'd never make a good preacher's wife; you know she is too mousy."

"On the contrary, I find she has every trait desirable in a wife." Clara's passion for helping to save the Rescue showed she had talents enough to organize and persuade. Not that he had thought of her in terms of qualifications since their kiss at the log.

"Now that I am here, she won't marry you if that is what you are waiting for. You know she always does whatever I ask." The fan flitted back and forth. Flirting. Definitely flirting.

"This isn't like climbing a tree to get your kitten down, or allowing you to wear her favorite dress. You can't tell her who to marry."

"Obviously not. If she really wanted you, she would have fought me for you. She had an entire year. All she had to do was step off the train and say, 'I do.' You would have figured out we'd changed places quickly enough."

Catherine's words pierced his heart. Did Clara want him as a husband? She hadn't approached the subject since the letter from her father. Nor had she pushed him away. He didn't have an answer.

"Clara would never allow her niece or nephew to be born without a father's name. She'll step aside for me."

"You assume too much. I have no desire to marry you. We do not suit on any level. Last year when I proposed, in my nervousness, I thought I was addressing your sister. Which you knew. Even if Clara never accepts my suit, I cannot, and will not, marry you."

Catherine switched from flirting to tears in a single blink. "Then what am I to do?"

"Hiramsville has no shortage of men seeking wives. If you only want a father for your child, I am sure many of them will oblige."

"You expect me to marry a man I've never met who is not of my station?"

"What station? This isn't Boston. There are only two kinds of men out there: the ones that work hard and the ones that don't. Find yourself one of the hardworking ones, and you'll never want for a roof over your head and food on the table."

"But everyone expects…"

Unbelievable. How had he ever thought his mistake had been God's will? "Catherine, have you written to your parents?"

"Of course not."

"I have written them several times. No one expects that you will marry me, because you are supposed to be married to a member of New York's nouveau riche. Only you disappeared. Your father has hired the Pinkertons. Although she hasn't said it, your sister has been worried sick over you. I have worried and prayed for you."

Catherine covered her face with her hands and made crying sounds. Her display might have softened another man's heart, but Lewis had been on the receiving end of her crocodile tears often enough to recognize them for what they were.

Reverend Green shifted in his seat.

"You can stop the theatrics. Your tears have never worked on me."

Catherine lifted her face from her hands. Not a speck of dampness on her face. "It was worth a try. Not that you or Clara will believe me, but I never intended this to go so far." She stood. "Good day, Lewis, and to you, Reverend."

Lewis closed the door behind her.

"That is the woman you were going to marry because you thought it was God's will?" asked Reverend Green.

"Unfortunately, yes."

"I hate to say this, but you were dumber than a box of rocks to think that. Not only is Clara better suited to the wife of a preacher, but she is also more suited to you. I have never seen twins who looked more alike and yet were so different."

"As children, they often switched places. I believe they confused their mother more than once. Clara usually gave the ruse away."

"I know it is none of my never mind, but does Clara know how deeply you care for her?"

"I've tried to tell her." The three words he'd spoken were not enough, nor were the kisses they'd shared.

"I think you'd better try harder or this one will talk her right on the next train out of town."

"My thoughts exactly. I trust you can get your own stew?"

Reverend Green grinned. "Run to her son."

⇒•◇•⇐

Emily let herself in the front door of Mrs. Reese's, blocking Clara's exit.

"Oh, I'm so glad you are here. Can you help them with the letters?" Clara's words tumbled out. She'd been waylaid by questions and still needed to find Lewis.

Emily paused and looked into Clara's eyes. "Is something wrong? Is it one of our friends?"

"Catherine is here. I must find Lewis."

"Here in the house?"

"Hannah's hotel." If only it wouldn't be rude to run out the door. Lewis must still be at the church.

"Reverend Green had a coughing fit. Reverend Staples took him home to feed him dinner."

The manse. Clara had never been there. It wouldn't be proper, even with the always-present chaperone. "Thank you. I'll be back to help as soon as I can."

"I'll be praying." Emily squeezed Clara's arm and smiled.

The friendly encouragement bolstered Clara as she raced down the street as fast as she could without raising her skirts. To save time, she cut through the alley behind the church and to the little house that, until an hour ago, might have one day been her home. Slowing her step, she took a deep breath and walked around to the front porch.

Reverend Green sat in his rocker. He raised a hand in greeting.

Relief filled her. She wouldn't have to knock on the door. "Is Lewis, I mean, Reverend Staples here?"

"I know who you mean, Miss Clara. He left not two minutes ago looking for you."

"He did?"

"Yes. We had a visitor. She looked quite a bit like you."

No. No. No. Clara was supposed to find him first. She turned.

"Come back." Reverend Green's call stopped her. "Wait here."

If only it was in her nature to be unlike what she'd been taught, she'd leave while other people spoke. Clara turned back. "I need to find him."

"And he wants to find you. Any second he will get to Mrs. Reese's and hear that you are looking for him and be back. I can't stand to watch the two of you run all over town missing each other because you took different shortcuts." Reverend Green pointed to the other chair. "Sit and catch your breath."

Seeing the wisdom in the reverend's suggestion, Clara joined him on the porch. "I can't believe my sister came here."

"She does look remarkably similar to you. I doubted Lewis's story about getting you two mixed up when he proposed. I can see how, if one of you tried to impersonate the other, you could have pulled it off."

"He told you?"

"Yes."

Clara wasn't sure what to say. She'd told Mrs. Reese. It must be natural to want advice from someone wiser.

Reverend Green chuckled.

Clara turned her head to see what was worthy of a laugh.

"I am imagining the looks on people's faces when they see your sister walking down the street. She looks so much like you but—"

Clara gasped and covered her mouth. There was nothing funny about her sister being mistaken for her. People would think...

"I didn't mean to upset you. No one is going to think she is you for very long or that the child is Lewis's. May I ask if you know when she will deliver?"

"Catherine said October." Catherine seemed large for a woman who had two months before the child arrived. Clara had so little experience in such things, that she was unsure.

"I'd reckon earlier than that."

The sound of running feet echoed in the porch rafters.

Reverend Green stood. "See, I told you he would come back."

"Clara." Lewis rounded the corner of the manse. He bent over and clutched his knees.

"Are you alright?"

Lewis shook his head as he stood, still gasping. "I …haven't …run …so …fast …"

Clara descended the steps. "Reverend Green said Catherine came here."

He nodded and put a hand on the porch railing to support himself.

"I know she thinks that she should be able to marry you because …well, everything. I'm not going to stand in the way of whatever decision you make. Emily told me of a job, Amanda wrote about needing an English teacher in the German school in Grunleuf. If you choose her, I'll leave. It will be better if I am not here. When I visit I'll do my best to pretend these last weeks didn't happen." Clara swallowed back the tears forming. "I don't want you to feel trapped. But Mrs. Reese told me I should fight for love if I found it. I think I have. My feelings have not changed since I told you I loved you by the river. If anything they have multiplied. I'm not going to turn this into another contest with Catherine. I just wanted you to know where I stood."

Lewis didn't respond.

He'd decided.

Her heart broke again.

Unable to keep looking at him, Clara turned away. She would take the train to Austin in the morning. Catherine would rail at her for not attending the wedding. She couldn't. Her feet propelled her down the path. *Don't look back. Don't look back.*

"Clara!" His shout covered the sound of his footsteps.

Lewis wrapped his hand around her arm and spun her to face him. His chest heaved as he grabbed her other arm, holding her in place.

Clara's heart raced as his lips descended to meet hers. This kiss was different than any other they shared, filled with a mix of passion, longing, and a hint of anger. The intensity stole her breath away. His arms encircled her, steadying her and drawing her closer, into a place of safety. Unbidden, she wrapped her arms around his neck and leaned into him with boldness she had never felt before. If this was to be her last kiss, she wanted it to go on forever.

Too soon he ended the kiss and rested his forehead on hers. "Clara, don't you dare leave," he growled softly. "I love you. Only you. You don't need to fight for me. I'm yours if you'll have me. I've written to your father to ask for his blessing. I had decided this afternoon—before Catherine came— that I couldn't wait any longer. Marry me? Be my wife and partner?"

He was proposing? This wasn't the end. She opened her mouth to reply.

"Miss Clara!" Donny ran around the church. "Miss Clara, Doc says to come quick!"

22

lara ran after Donny around the church and out of sight. Having barely caught his breath from running from Mrs. Reese's and then their kiss, Lewis prayed he had a bit more strength left and followed. Donny stood at the edge of the road, waving and yelling. Clara slowed her pace. Lewis caught up, and they joined Donny.

TJ drove the doctor's buggy toward them. He slowed to a stop and reached down a hand for Clara.

"What's wrong?"

"It's your sister," said TJ.

There wasn't enough room for three in the small contraption.

"I'll be there in a minute." Lewis waved TJ on.

Donny matched his steps with Lewis. "Miss Clara was not easy to find. I should have known you'd be sparking. Did you know her sister was here? I nearly swallowed my butterscotch whole when I saw her. They look so much alike. I knew she wasn't Clara right quick on account of her being with child."

"Why did the doctor send for Clara?"

"Miss Clara's sister fainted right there in the middle of the boardwalk in front of the mercantile. Mr. Tarr wants me to scrub off the blood. But I told him finding Miss Clara was more important, and I couldn't take the job." Donny turned into an alleyway.

Confident the kid knew all the best shortcuts, Lewis didn't hesitate to follow him. "Blood?"

"She hit her head real hard."

Lewis's breath became labored so he stopped asking questions. The doctor's buggy wasn't outside his office. TJ must have come and gone.

"Bye, Preacher." Donny waved and continued down the street. Then he stopped and ran back. Donny held out a crumpled telegram. "I almost forgot. I was taking this to you when Miss Clara's sister ... Don't tell them it was late, please."

"I won't. I'd say finding Miss Clara was more important than whatever is in here."

Donny rushed off again.

Lewis smoothed out the envelope on his leg. He didn't need more bad news today. The top line listed the wire's origin as Boston.

> **Wed with my blessing.**
> **Letter to follow.**
> **C. Taylor**

The best news he could have had, given the time for a telegram to arrive, Mr. Taylor would have given his permission prior to his proposal ...which still awaited an answer.

Lewis climbed the stairs to Dr. Palmer's. No one sat in the small outer office.

The exam room door was closed. Lewis walked upstairs to the room Jax occupied. The door was also closed. Across the hall, the door to Miss Lavender's room stood ajar. Hushed voices talked within. Lewis tapped on the door.

Miss Petunia answered. "Evening, Reverend."

She opened the door further. Three other women from the Rescue sat in chairs around Lavender's bed.

"Have you seen Clara?" he asked.

"She is downstairs with Doc and her sister." Petunia looked at the other women. "We were praying."

"Do you know what is wrong?"

The women either shrugged their shoulders or shook their heads.

"I'll wait downstairs then." Lewis returned to the small waiting room.

Mrs. Reese entered. "I just heard the news. How is Clara's sister?"

"I don't know." Lewis pointed to the closed door. "No one has come out."

Mrs. Reese sat beside him and pulled out her knitting. "Were you able to speak with Clara before disaster struck."

"For a moment." Not long enough for her to answer. An inkling of doubt poked at him. She wouldn't say no again, would she?

⎯⎯⟫•◆•⟪⎯⎯

Dr. Palmer placed the last stitch closing the cut above Catherine's left eyebrow, while Clara held her unconscious sister's hand.

"Doctor." The nurse behind Clara called his attention to something, communicating with her eyes.

"Clara, I need to examine your sister more fully." With a small set of scissors, he cut the thread. He set the needle and scissors back on a tray. "The nurse will be in here with me. If you will wait outside, I believe I heard someone else arrive, so you will not be alone."

"I can stay. We are twins…"

The nurse laid a hand on Clara's back. "Dr. Palmer needs the space to work. We will tell you if anything changes or if she wakes up."

Clara searched Dr. Palmer's face. Seeing nothing other than compassion in the doctor's eyes, she nodded. He would do his best. In the few days they courted, she learned he cared for his patients more than anything. Reluctantly, she left the room, closing the door behind her.

From his place on the wooden bench next to Mrs. Reese, Lewis stood.

"How is she?" asked Mrs. Reese.

"She is unconscious. Dr. Palmer said he needed to examine her more." Tears she'd held back in the exam room crept over the dam she'd put up.

Lewis opened his arms, and Clara walked into them. He held her as she silently wept, her tears soaking through his shirt.

Mrs. Reese patted Clara's hand in comfort, but it was Lewis who spoke up first.

"Dr. Palmer is good at what he does." His voice was soft and reassuring as he gently stroked her hair and held her close.

Clara took deep breaths to gather herself before pulling away.

Mrs. Reese stood up. "Why don't I get us some tea? Dr. Palmer keeps a kettle in his kitchen. I could use a cup myself."

Clara nodded. "That would be lovely."

Mrs. Reese gave them one last smile before heading out of the room to fetch their drinks.

Lewis sat down next to Clara on the bench and placed an arm around her shoulders in comfort.

"I'm scared," Clara admitted, her voice quivered. "I barely got her back. My telegram probably hasn't even reached my parents yet."

Lewis used both hands to cup her face and looked deep into her eyes. "Look at me."

She searched his eyes and found comfort.

"Have faith."

A tear rolled down her face. He thumbed it away.

"I do have faith. Faith doesn't prevent bad things from happening."

"No, but it brings hope that somehow the future that God sees, will be the one tailored for us. And everything will turn for our good." Lewis didn't give any false platitudes.

Catherine's future wasn't any more in Clara's hands than it had ever been, even those few hours when she pretended to be her twin.

When Dr. Palmer exited the exam room, his face didn't give anything away. He pulled over a ladder-back chair. "Your sister woke up."

Clara moved out of Lewis's embrace to stand.

Dr. Palmer stopped her with a hand on her arm. "Not yet. I am concerned about the child she is carrying. Catherine has not been eating or sleeping well, and the train travel has taken its toll on her. I want her to stay here for the next few days. I need you to convince her that staying is in her best interest."

"I'll do my best."

"I'll rearrange things upstairs so we can put her with Miss Lavender." Dr. Palmer turned to Lewis. "Let's go put that healed hand of yours to good use."

An hour later, Catherine was settled into Lavender's room to stay the night. Clara said her goodbyes, leaving Catherine in the capable hands of Dr. Palmer's nurse who had already chased all the other visitors out.

Only Lewis remained downstairs. "Mrs. Reese sent word to Hannah that the room is not needed. I told her I would see you home."

She took his arm and allowed him to guide her down the street.

Clara paused to stare at the sky awash in a beautiful array of oranges and pink, bidding the sun goodnight. "It is amazing how the sky doesn't reflect any of the panic I've felt today."

"The day has been rather full." Lewis turned down a street near the river that would lead them the longest way home.

The idea that he wished to prolong their time together made her smile, then stop mid-stride.

Lewis turned to her. "What is wrong?"

"I never answered you. Your proposal." Clara covered her mouth with her hand and was not sure which of the battling emotions was showing on her face. The urge to giggle won.

His eyebrows rose. "Well?"

Clara took a deep breath and let the words out slowly. "Yes. Yes, I will marry you."

Lewis gave her a smile that was pure triumph. He wrapped his arms around her waist and swung her in a circle. When he set her back down, he pulled away from the embrace but kept his hands on her waist. His lips were gentle, tender. Like the sunset, they promised a better tomorrow and thousands more after that.

The kiss lasted a few moments before Lewis pulled away. He brushed his thumb lightly over her bottom lip. "Let's get you home."

The sun had set completely now, leaving just the faint twinkle of stars to light their way. Clara wondered if she should tell him her home wasn't in a big old house filled to bursting, but in his arms. Perhaps that would be a sentence best uttered after they wed.

Epilogue

everend Staples! Reverend Staples!" Donny's shout cut through the early morning bustle.

A thousand thoughts ran through Lewis's mind as the boy approached. Who had sent him? The doctor? Was Catherine dead? Did Clara need him?

Donny stopped in front of him and held out a telegram. "I didn't bend it this time. It is addressed to you and Miss Clara. The operator told me to give it to you and have you deal with things."

Considering the telegraph operator knew the contents of the message, he would be in a position to give such advice.

Lewis dug a nickel out of his pocket. "Do you know where Clara is?"

Donny put the coin in his pouch. "She was walking to Doc's a few minutes ago."

Lewis hurried to Dr. Palmer's. The nurse sat in the outer office.

"Miss Clara?"

The nurse pointed to the floor above her. "We put her sister

235

in with Miss Lavender. I sure hope Dr. Palmer convinces the town they need a hospital soon."

Lewis took the steps two at a time.

Jax's door was open, but the room was dark. Lewis looked in only long enough to see that the man was sleeping before knocking on the door across the hall.

Clara answered, only opening the door a few inches. "Lewis, it is early for a visit."

Lewis lowered his voice hoping it wouldn't carry. "I was looking for you."

She waved him back and turned to address the room. "It is for me. I'll be back in a minute. Yes, I'll ask the nurse for some clean water."

Opening the door only wide enough to squeeze through, Clara stepped into the hall. "What do you need?"

"There is a telegram to both of us."

"Let's go downstairs to read it. I need to talk to the nurse anyway."

The nurse went back to the kitchen area, leaving Lewis and Clara alone.

"Shall we open it here?" she asked.

Lewis pointed to the long wooden bench. They sat shoulder to shoulder as Lewis opened the telegram.

> **Coming to Texas, arrive next week.**
> **Want to be at wedding.**
> **Will take C home.**
> *Mr. C Taylor*

"What wedding? Which C?" asked Clara.

Lewis pulled last night's telegram from his pocket. "I wrote to your father the morning Reverend Whitesides left. I wanted his permission to marry you, even if I was demoted to a clerk or lost my job."

"That is what you mailed that day."

"Yes. I got the answer last night. Donny had it in his pocket when he was looking for you."

"So, you didn't know that you had my father's blessing when you proposed?"

"No. I didn't. But even if he hadn't given it, I wanted to marry you."

Clara blushed and kissed his cheek. "I see I have converted you to my way of thinking."

"I am a believer." Lewis leaned in, and she closed her eyes, welcoming his kiss. He kept it short since anyone could walk into the room and see them. He pulled away and ran his thumb over her lips, caressing them gently. "I love you, Clara."

Her blush deepened. A lifetime with Clara would be too short.

Historical Notes:

While looking through historical newspapers for the summer of 1880 in the Dallas-Fort Worth area, I found the story, reported in, of the two-headed chicken. Assuming the article is true, it is one of those truths that is stranger-than-fiction moments.

If I was to make a batch of jumble cakes today, my children would call them cookies. I have found several recipes and most don't contain leavening agents and snap like a wafer. Around the 1600s and by 1880, they evolved to have fruits and even nuts in them.

Although I don't name it, some of my readers may have picked up on the reference to Texas Christian University which started in the town of Thorpe Spring as AddRan College in 1873. The school was taken over by the Disciples of Christ in 1890. They transferred its operations to Waco in 1896, and its name eventually changed to Texas Christian University and was moved to Fort Worth. Any rumors of the college moving in 1880 are simply that, rumors created by the author.

In 1880, Thorpe Spring had one thousand residents—more than five times the population it has today. The natural sulfur springs attracted many people to their healing waters. Since using the real town doesn't suit my needs or fit with the imaginary Hiramsville, I have given it a historical nod by simply calling it the Springs.

As noted in the other books in this series, Bradford College's curriculum was quite advanced and difficult. However the addition of a nursing class was my own invention.

Acknowledgments

Thanks to my assistant, Mara, who has become a dear friend, for pushing me to write. Without Mara this book and others wouldn't exist. She deserves far more than a book dedication, but as an avid reader I hope she loves it.

As always, thanks to Tammy, Nanette, Julie, Jori, and Cami who are so willing to help make all my projects better. I would never make it through a day without Maria, Nichole and Cindy whose texts and messages keep me writing.

Big thanks to Maria for the excellent edits. And to my excellent proofreaders who are not to be blamed for any remaining errors. Thank you all!

My family, for sharing their home with the fictional characters who often get fed better than they did. Seriously I haven't cooked in a year. And my husband who encourages me every crazy step of the way.

And to my Father in Heaven for putting these wonderful people, and any I may have forgotten to mention, in my life. I am grateful for every experience and blessing I have been granted.

About the Author

orin Grace was born in Colorado and has been moving around the country ever since, living in eight states and several imaginary worlds. She holds a degree in graphic design which comes in handy with creating book covers. Currently, she lives with her husband, and a dog who is insanely jealous of her laptop.

When not writing, Lorin enjoys creating graphics, visiting historical sites, museums, painting furniture, texting emojies to her children, and reading. Three of her books, her debut novel, *Waking Lucy* (2017), *Mending Fences* (2018), and *Not the Bodyguard's Baby* (2020) have won Recommend Read awards in the League of Utah Writers Published book contest.